NIGHTSWALLOW

Bronwen Winter Phoenix

To David
I've always admired
your work!
Best wishes
love
Bronwen W Phoenix

Copyright

Published in 2008 by YouWriteOn.com

Copyright © Text Bronwen Winter Phoenix

First Edition

Published by YouWriteOn.com

Acknowledgements

Although I got most of this story from my own warped subconscious mind (in other words, a dream), I would like to thank my mum, for reading and proofreading purposes; my Tim, for listening to me when I wake him up at 3am with a great draft/idea and lastly Catherine, just for listening.

Chapter One

I am Night. Do not misunderstand me - that is my name, not some overcooked statement referring to what I am - a spirit of the dark. My name is Night Swallow - simply a name given to me when I was still alive.

When I passed over to the dark side of the world, a place void of daylight, I was just twenty-six years of age. A series of unusual events led up to my murder, which took place back home in London. I had returned to my old home there to forget these events, but unfortunately the nightmare caught up with me a little too late.

A lot has happened since then and my understanding of my surroundings has flourished, along with my pain.

Although I am rested now, I wait for a time when things will become clear to me again - perhaps all at once, when the clouding of my heart is dissolved into the mysterious light that I have seen envelope many others into its core.

I don't claim to understand this light, but I wish for it to take me like it has taken the others.

In life I was a journalist and a lone female traveller. Always without rest I rushed through life looking for the latest story as if searching for answers to all I could never know or understand; turning them into questions, always searching for more.

My lifestyle was hectic in busy, crowded London but it was only more recently that I began to crave new sights and sounds; to explore the world in a way I could capture in words and photographs. My digital camera and ultra-light laptop became my most prized possessions in a world that just kept on spinning; and like the world, I was on a merry-go-round unable to stop.

Throughout my travels I never faltered as I wrote down

every feeling, every new discovery, folk lore, ancient charm or latest craze; my articles were just starting to become well-respected in the world of travel journalism. I don't want to be a cliché but it was like I had found my passion, my calling, a small treasure box filled with light and possiblities. But it was all mine and mine alone.

New worlds seemed to open up to me, filling my mind with new doors and walkways, windows to new, exotic places – and at the same time taking away older ones.
I began to feel more isolated from my old life as the days passed in beautiful sunsets, blood orange and red blotting the skies. I was an observer, a loner.

I tried to keep in touch with my friends, even a couple of lovers but it seemed that the more time I spent losing myself in travel, the more distant I grew not only in terms of shores but also in mentality.

Gone was the old fascination in the London club scene, days I spent managing to score free tickets to the latest new bar or trying out whatever new cocktail was in fashion, getting drunk with friends and shopping for the ridiculously expensive but hellishly sexy little cocktail dresses and perfectly pointed heels. I swapped them for rugged old denim shorts and threadbare tops without giving a damn about how I looked to my new world. Because it didn't give a damn about me.

It beckoned me, opened up to me like a rose slowly blooming in the palm of my hand, swallowing me whole. And I could feel it.

I seemed to delve into something far deeper and more meaningful than anything I'd had before, yet the deeper I got the darker my depression seemed to haunt me, taking me over like a dark sea sweeping over my old life; the things I had left behind.

I dwelled on these thoughts while sipping cappuccinos in the stylish coffee houses of Prague, went wild in the vibrant night clubs of Barcelona and explored the ancient tombs of Egypt, dark, musty and foreboding. For once I was truly alive.

For a short time I shopped in New York, stepping in and out of yellow taxi cabs and making an obscene amount of fake friends who loved the idea of my career more than me when the truth was I was struggling to afford the rent, eating beans on toast or starving more nights than not. Yet I was still an outsider.

The city soon lost its appeal, the wave of noisy people almost drowning me in their click-clacking shoes, their endless mobile ringtones, the shouts of the weak and the powerful.

I felt as if one day I would slip through the sidewalks, never to be seen again yet no-one would even notice or care.

I found myself transfixed by the luminous signs that filled the Tokyo night scene, ordering food that I could neither establish as being animal or vegetable – taking my chances with the menu before stepping onto the tube to visit beautiful temples and observe the ceremonies of the monks, shivering at the strength of their faith and wishing for some faith of my own. I was vaguely aware of that search, but answers never came to me the way others had been blessed.

I relaxed on the beautiful white beaches of Malaysia, hoping to let my inner self catch up with my body and feeling strangely empty at the end of each day, watching on the beach as the sun went down, bathing me in its orange light. But at the same time I felt disconnected, hollow, I craved the company – if only to see what I had been missing. It was then I began to set my sights on Thailand.

In Bangkok I browsed the Chatuchat and Water Gate markets, took in the nightlife while avoiding the dull bars that still dominated the city, and met many friendly people who offered me more drugs than I could ever need.

My photographs echoed my feelings at the time, so very alive but still restless, taking new angles and capturing the revellers who seemed to be content and immersed in their surroundings, laughing and stumbling through the night streets the way they stumbled through lovers, friends, life.

It was not a place for a lonely traveller, or maybe it was

just me – always the outsider. Either way, I quickly got bored of the Thai capital and headed out to the more exotic locations...an interesting venture to the Satun islands. That was when I first saw the island that took my breath away.

When I first reached the golden shores, it pulled me in completely. Whatever part of me that had resisted wandering just gave in, and at once I knew that I wanted to explore and to be alone, to savagely take apart every experience and absorb it into my being.

When I first got to the island, lonely and private it seemed to be calling to me. I knew I had to stay the night there. That is where my end began, as it were, and where this story originally started.

Yet there is much more to my past than I can remember; it comes to me in flashes of my far-distant life. Sometimes I think that I forget the most important details, instead opting for the more alluring parts of my experiences that still glimmer in my mind like gold dust. Sometimes I wonder if I was there for a reason, as if the island called me there like it was my destiny. Either way, the things I saw and heard there sealed my fate for what feels like an eternity.

I think that first and foremost, it is important to learn what I am now, and what made me this way.

The start of me, this form as I am now began when I had moved back into my small apartment in London town and was finding it hard to 'settle' after my ordeal on the island - the courts, the lonely turmoil and fear. I was glad to be back with friends, although they barely recognised me after such a long time away.

My once-pale skin had now been baked with a deep tan, my hair much longer and unruly, and my personality quieter, more contemplative than when I had left. As I ate my comfort food - vegetable lasagne while in front of my wide screen plasma - I no longer felt much like myself but instead changed.

I was still skinny from all the exploring and the odd sick spot I managed to catch while eating something that wasn't quite suited to my palate; Thai squid for example. I should have been overjoyed at being able to shop, at last in posh London stores for the tiny sized clothing I'd once wanted, but instead I stayed at home, writing down my memories.

It seemed like a good idea to lock myself in a dark room and just write, yet the things I ended up writing were entirely unplanned; as if I had taken a part of something back with me, brought it into my home.

I had already received a publishing deal on the story of my travels and what I had experienced in Thailand, earning me enough money to relax for a while. Yet every time I placed myself in front of the screen, I felt an overwhelming urge to continue writing the strange fiction I had started for the first time on the island. Had it blessed me this strange gift? Or was it a curse?

Before I left London, fiction writing had been impossible to me, yet now it flowed deeply, strangely through my fingers onto the keys, always disturbing thoughts that beckoned my mind into darker places.

I could become absorbed deep into the story, my fingers barely pausing I had no time to think, yet the words... the words flowed almost as if from somewhere else entirely.

I'd look up and hours had passed since I'd sat down. My green tea would be stone cold, and darkness would have stealthily crept into the room.

When I passed over to the dark – and it is dark here, yet always beautiful in my superhuman eyes – my passing was not by any means peaceful.

And just when I thought I was over the nightmare, a new one began when my life was cruelly taken from me. Now, I linger in the spirit world until I can find a cure for my curse. I am Night.

Chapter Two

I awoke from what seemed like a long and deep sleep, to find myself in utter darkness. There was a blank, cold feeling in my heart and at once I knew that I was dead. I found myself centimetres away from my apartment wall, staring blankly into the dark.

My eyes were wide open and slowly my mind began to fill with vivid memories of what had happened. I allowed myself a moment to begin to function again.

I lazily moved my fingers which were now pressed against the cool, dark wall. I was in my apartment, a place no more familiar to me than anywhere I could have filled with furniture and called home.

Nothing had ever seemed settled, especially with the suitcases that sat prominently around the house, still holding trinkets from my many travels. It was an apartment more often used as storage space, not like a home at all.

But this was my home, and I was aware that nothing had changed in it. The gentle hum of my computer in the background brought me back to reality and I soon realised the sense of panic rising up inside me like desperation; I cannot explain this feeling, apart from a horrible coldness in my heart.

My first instinct seemed immediately impossible, but nevertheless I began to rise up the wall. The higher I got, the more the panic seized all the nerves in my body. I knew I was scared, but I could not figure out why. When I reached the second floor, the sight of the large window looking out into the night's sky soothed me slightly.

The silence filling my apartment frightened me, and I knew I was looking for something. A memory so far away in my mind, I heard a voice telling me to look for the bright lights in the night sky.

But there were no bright lights; I could not see the moon and all the stars looked dead: black, gone, vanished from the darkness. I absently imagined them to be dead, possibly as an association to myself. I rose higher; ascending through the ceilings that seamlessly passed through my body.

I was in a strange place now, but all the darkness felt the same, the feeling of panic, of need. I began to feel a sense of anxiety, a sudden dread of something pulling me higher, further into someplace unknown. I resisted the urge to cling to something solid.

I was on the second floor of a stranger's apartment; I could not stand the dark any longer. Quickly I reached out for the light, knowing exactly where it was. Switching it on was no problem. As soon as I had done, I felt my whole body jolt. Staring back at me was a figure in the living room.

His vivid green eyes met mine; a man in a long black coat with dark green trousers that looked more like elegant rags. He was holding a cigarette, standing against the wall in a relaxed manner.

The room around him was completely bare; not even carpet remained. The walls were marked and old, the hall that I stood in looked dark and damp, and also slightly warped. My full attention however, was on this man. Somehow I had reached an understanding that he was like me: dead. He beckoned me towards him.

Trembling, I slowly encouraged myself to move towards this strange figure. To my eyes, he looked mysterious and yet somehow beautiful, and I wondered where this creature had come from. He looked at me, then at the cigarette and smiled, amused.

"Cigarette?" His first words to me. I declined the offer; I'd always been a non-smoker.

"I thought as much, a bit pointless really. Lighting one seems to relax me. Funny how something I'd clung to as a mortal now brings an almost childlike comfort to me in these times."

At first I failed to understand, then suddenly it came to me: of course, he could not inhale the smoke.

I did not - could not - say a word. I sat on the window ledge, completely taken in by the figure before me, his raven black hair shining in the moonlight.

We stayed like that for a while. It seemed like the most perfectly comfortable and natural thing to do. The feeling of panic was already gone, fading fast from my mind. I realised I had a lot of questions.

"I watched it happen, you know. Your death," his voice shocked me, breaking through the silence so harshly. I turned to him, speechless at what he'd said. His green eyes pierced mine and I felt completely helpless.

Then in a litany of flashbacks and horrendous thoughts, I remembered what had happened to me in my last moments of struggle.

He continued, "I was waiting for you, hoping... you'd find me."

The sense of loss shattered the numbness for me. I began to find the situation so horrible, so...unfair, I felt like screaming. I had an overwhelming desire to race down to my former apartment and confront my blood-drained corpse.

"You know, that wouldn't be such a good idea..." The mysterious gentleman's soft velvety voice filled the room adequately enough to calm me for a moment.

Turning to him, I looked him straight in the eye and spoke my first words: "Who are you?"

"My name is Magnus."

I knew from that moment that he could not answer my questions. He could not tell me how long he had been there for, or why. All he knew was that it was always dark.

Sometimes I wonder if I am still in the same place, or if I have somehow moved sideways instead of up or down; the ways you are supposed to move when you die.

Who knows, my memories of Magnus are some of the most beautiful I can remember, my past life; a tainted, haunting mystery that comes to me in flashes of light - it taunts me as I rediscover pieces of my youth or passion-filled moments where it seemed like my heart would never stop beating.

After the first time together, his presence was there always for me. I did not feel that same panic I had felt when I awoke in this strange new place, I did not feel loneliness or sorrow, apart from fleeting thoughts and haunting memories of my time to die. His presence soothed me, warmed my soul and made me do things I never thought I would do.

That first night, I literally took flight, my soul or whatever it should be called, solid entity or invisible being (I tend to think the latter) took flight into the night air. I had left Magnus behind temporarily; I had no fear of being lost.

It became an urge building inside of me, and instantly he seemed to know what it was, and nodded. As I stepped up to the window it blew open, cold air blowing into the bare room. I stepped forward and without fear knew exactly what I wanted: to fly.

Unaware of how exactly to do this, I prepared myself before stepping into the air when an amazing feeling suddenly took over my body, propelling me forward like an instinct that had been buried deep inside; another secret perhaps so ancient it was deep-rooted somewhere in my soul. I soared that first night, and nothing had ever felt so wonderful.

The feeling at first was dizzying, the sharpness of movement required no effort from me, as all restrictions of my solid body had been so far removed from what I had become. I discovered I could cover large distances in the flash of an eye; I could see so much of what I'd wanted to see when I was alive, brief feelings of adventure had now come true for me. I saw the world with new, better eyes.

As I flew in the cold night air something else occurred to me; I wondered about God, for the first time since my death. Apart from Magnus I had not seen any such kind as me; I had seen nothing out of the ordinary. No lights.

The memory of being told to look for lights seemed to linger inside of me, bothering me slightly. I did not seem to know where it had come from. I had a sense of taking in the air, and it felt so wonderful to me. Like someplace foreign and different. At no time did I ever feel unsafe, and I did not feel in danger of falling to the ground.

My long chiffon dress blew around me in the cool night sky, my hair swept around my face and I had never felt so exhilarated. The stars shone now, lighting up the sky and making the moment beautiful.

My soul felt cleansed, my body felt strong and I had love in my heart for every living thing. I felt no mourning for whatever my past life had been, to be honest; I can only ever remember fragments of it. These fragments only started to bother me later on, and the world has changed so much since my death.

Returning to Magnus at last, he looked tired and worn. Slumped against the same wall, I saw a shiver escape him.

"I'm back," I said, my words feeling out of place in the cold, empty room. He looked up, undisturbed by my entrance.

"After a while of being here," his voice whispered, miserably, "things tend to come back to you. We find it difficult to go on having fun and games…"

"Why don't you tell me, why are we here, Magnus? Are there others?" I had many questions, but something stopped me from mentioning the urge to look for the lights.

"An inquisitive one. You were a journalist, no?" His accent was hard to place, perhaps a hint of French in there somewhere, I thought to myself as I continued to look into those mesmerising green eyes.

He solemnly shook his head, but instinct told me it was not an answer to my questions, rather a reply to my 'innocence' on the matter. Later, when I had time to mull over his behaviour and tiredness I understood that he did not have to be there for me, but instead chose to be. To me, his actions spoke far more to me that night than words ever could.

"I think perhaps you need to get out of this stuffy room," I'd told him, my ignorance shining through. I was taking his behaviour lightly, full of my new-found freedom with no need to think of reality and my old world. Although later I learned what he meant when he used those words of difficulty…of things coming back on you.

The smile faded from my face; he looked very tired, his eyes dull. He always looked very shaded in the moonlight, his pale skin looked almost grey and lifeless. This was one of the only times I'd known Magnus to act as if he had so little of self left in him - as if something had taken part of his spirit.

Chapter Three

As I tossed and turned in the tiny hotel room in Bangkok, I regretted ordering the Thai squid earlier. My skin was hot and clammy, the air conditioner had stopped working hours ago and I felt so incredibly alone. Not for the first time.

The mattress was ridiculously soft and as I realised there was absolutely no chance of me getting to sleep that night, I tried to wrench myself out of bed without throwing up - a tough feat but I managed it.

I needed water, and stumbling towards the window I found the tumbler I'd left there earlier. Gulping it down I felt the movements in my gut and quickly hurled myself towards the bathroom. So it begins, I thought as I let my sickness take control of my body.

It was the first time I'd ever felt really scared for my health, the fact that I was in Bangkok on my own with little or no help made me realise just how much I missed him.

I had briefly thought of Alex before in the last few months, but had never committed myself to picking up a phone due to a lack of what…confidence? No, that wasn't it. Perhaps I had just learned to block out my feelings, after all we hadn't been in a proper relationship for a couple of years by this time.

Things had never run smoothly for us; every time we got together it seemed we were waiting for the time-bomb to go off. The thing was, I'd never loved anyone so much or endured so much hurt from just one person. We hurt each other; it was an awkward but at the same time pure kind of love. I never said it was healthy.

By the time I'd managed to detach myself from the dirty bathroom floor, stomach muscles aching and in desperate need of a fresh drink, I finally found the strength to reach for the phone. I tried to remember his face, exactly as it had been the last time I saw him – and failed.

My hand trembled as I listened to the phone connecting to the other end, then hearing each ring and willing him to pick up. I was beginning to give up, about to hang up the receiver when he answered.

"Hello?" Alex's voice down the chunky plastic phone filled me with the warmth that I desperately needed. I stuttered, unable to form the correct words.

"Who is this?" He asked.

"It's me, it's Night," I replied. There was silence on his end, before he spoke up sounding very surprised and did I detect a hint of awkwardness?

"Night! What a surprise, where are you? Are you…are you okay?" He asked.

"Yeah, I'm okay. I'm in Bangkok, I was feeling a bit off and I just realised that I felt so…"

I trailed off as I heard giggling in the background, and a female voice asked who was calling.

"Oh, sorry, I'm listening please carry on," said Alex, sounding a little confused at my call. I heard the girl mutter at the other end.

"No, it's okay I can tell you're busy with…" I told him, sounding more than a little dejected.
"Ermmm…that's Sara, my girlfriend. We've been together about two months now. I would have told you, only you seem to have disappeared off the face of the earth…" He sounded almost cold now, and his words pierced through my heart: I could literally feel a pang there.

"Okay, look, I've got to go. Take care." I hung up the phone before he could say anything else.

A single tear fell down my cheek as I sat crouched by the window, tenderly holding my aching stomach and feeling more alone than ever. It was then that I wondered exactly what I was doing there.

I obviously wasn't missed, Alex had moved on and whether it was my fault or not was debatable. Surely it was childish of me to leave him for so long and still expect him to be there for me?

I'm not sure what brought on the tear; whether it was the tiny amount of emotion I'd allowed to trickle out of me, or the sheer numbness I felt in my detachment from everything I used to know so well.

I knew I had brought all of this on myself, and as I sat looking out into the busy night streets of the city, I knew I wanted to escape. As I ran my fingers through my knotted hair, I thought of the love that I'd lost long ago with a kind of fresh mourning I'd never expected to be there; it was like waking from a dream.

It was then I made up my mind to go south, somewhere away from all the noise…in the streets, in my head, somewhere I could finally figure out what I wanted. I needed to know who I was, because I didn't think I could recognise myself anymore; find myself in all the mess that layered my mind.

I arrived in Satun, known for its picturesque islands and beaches, via bus two days later. Although it was early in the morning, it was hot and I'd travelled far south of the city of angels, hoping to work things out in my mind. I was still slightly weak from the sickness episode and the fact I'd had some sleepless nights, but I was already feeling better in mentality.

It did not take me long to find a cheap hostel and when I reached my room, decided I was happy to find it was, so far, empty. It was a small room with only two beds, the window overlooking some dying grass and old buildings surrounded by a bright blue sky.

After I'd placed my bag down on the floor, I practically collapsed onto one of the beds and rested for a good few hours, allowing sleep to finally reach me and chase away my thoughts of loneliness. In between patches of dreams I was vaguely aware of laughter down the hall, and I barely registered that other travellers had also joined the hostel although thankfully, sharing a room.

Halfway through I remember getting out of bed and walking through the narrow corridor to the toilets, feeling woozy and to be blunt, out of it. To this day I can't remember if it was a dream or reality but as I splashed cold water onto my face I looked into the mirror and immediately saw someone standing behind me.

It appeared to be an elderly man with long, unruly grey hair and a bearded face with piercing but almost ill-looking amber eyes. His skin was aged badly and he appeared to be topless, nevertheless regal and decorated in a way that looked traditional but really, I didn't have a clue. His chest bore a tattoo of what was once a great eagle, although now it looked old and pathetic, faded and wrinkled.

I took all this in within just a couple of seconds, before stumbling and clumsily looking round to see why this man was looking at me in such a strange manner. But there was no-one there, just an empty bathroom with muddy footprints across the floor. I must have found my way back to bed and into a deep sleep because I cannot remember the episode too clearly.

When I woke up properly, it was around noon which meant I'd been asleep for six hours. After a shower and a fresh change of clothes I ventured out of the hostel and into the blinding sun, quickly covering my eyes with the cheap sunglasses I'd bought back in Bangkok.

The hostel was only minutes from a beautiful, white sand beach and turquoise sea and I walked barefoot over the hot sand. Although the scene was, arguably, picturesque, the beach was far from empty as other travellers and locals relaxed on the sands. Some local men were playing with a pink rubber ball; they smiled at me as I walked past.

My stomach had started to grumble when, further up the beach I found a small bar and café and made the decision to have my first proper meal since the food poisoning. As I looked at the menu, I smiled up at a man of large build with beautiful dark skin and toned muscles.

He wore a red vest and had shoulder-length black dreadlocks, with deep brown eyes and perfect skin. He smiled at me and motioned a question; could he sit? I nodded.

"Hey there, I have not seen you around before," he spoke in a deeply accented voice yet seemed to speak almost perfect English.

"Yes, I just got here this morning," I replied, mildly curious of the person who now sat across from me at the small table. He acknowledged my London accent and reached across to shake my hand, something I wasn't expecting but firmly grasped his hand back; I could tell he was very strong.

"I am Mandely, but you can call me Mandi," he said as he looked into my eyes. I could tell at once he was very open and friendly, which at once set me at ease and sparked my curiosity.

"My name's Night, nice to meet you," I responded. His expression said it all.

"Night, huh? That's a very unusual name; I'd say by your eyes it suits you."

Many people had commented on my unusual grey eyes, yet I was not expecting 'Mandi' to say such a thing and it took me by surprise. I smiled at the unexpected comment, not really sure how to reply.

He began to tell me about himself and I found out some very interesting facts: he was a local, a guide born just down the coast. His father had been a fisherman who'd died at sea when he was just five years old and thinking back he could remember his shape more than his face; a giant hulk of a man who always brought giant fish back to the small household cottage he lived in with his family.

I listened, intrigued by the confident but humble tones of his voice, his mannerisms, the way he looked at me almost shyly, but in a playful way I couldn't quite place. Was he flirting?

Finding myself in a conversation with someone so open, I couldn't help but feel I had to offer something in return. So I told him about me, why I was travelling, the things I wrote about and what interested me about Thailand. But after a couple of minutes of speaking, I realised I wanted to tell him the real reason I was here; there was something about speaking to a stranger – no it wasn't even that, it was him - that allowed me to open up. He watched me intently as the words unexpectedly poured from my lips, and I even surprised myself.

When I had finished, he opened his mouth to reply, But then the waiter finally came to take my order and Mandi stood up to leave for work.

"Night, can I invite you out for dinner tonight? I'd like to know more about you," he asked, almost as if sensing I had more to say to him. I accepted, my curiosity well and truly awakened by this surprisingly charming man.

As I sat overlooking the beach, eating my tropical-style omelette and observing the people that walked by, I thought I felt a change somewhere deep down in my mind.

I spent the rest of the day on the beach, observing the view of the islands in the distance and resting on the warm sands. I picked up a single shell that looked almost pure white as I made my way along the shore, enjoying the warm sun on my back.

I found myself stepping cautiously into the turquoise blue sea, letting the water come up to my waist without a single care in the world. It cleansed me as I shut my eyes and subconsciously held onto the shell in my hand, breathing in the clear air. I smiled as I felt the sun warming my skin, deepening my tan and taking me further away from the pale of my past.

I had always been fair, yet now I was almost unrecognisable when I looked in the mirror, my grey eyes still the same as ever.

I stayed in the sea for about half an hour, basking in the golden sun and watching the small fish that occasionally swam around me as if welcoming me in an odd, fish-type way. The water was lukewarm but refreshing as I looked once more upon the islands that seemed to scatter around the sea.

They had already taken my attention, my mind beginning to work out the idea that they were exactly what I needed.

By the end of the day, I had made up my mind that I wanted to visit at least one of them; the thought of a small quiet island seemed like the ideal place to gather my thoughts of what to do next.

I knew I would ask Mandi about it that night at dinner; he was taking me to some little restaurant as part of the 'guide service' that he had to offer me. It did occur to me as strange; maybe he felt my isolation or just wanted to take me on a date. Either way it was an interesting way to meet someone. I couldn't hide it; he'd charmed me.

With that thought I headed back to the hostel to wash the sea out of my hair and change into one of my still half-decent dresses, noticing that it fitted much more loosely than I had remembered. As I combed my unruly hair I felt a slight flutter in my stomach as I prepared to ask my complimentary guide about visiting the islands.

Chapter Four

How many words will it take to explain what has happened in the long time I have been of this side of the dark? I cannot tell, but every word is like the blood pouring out of me that fateful night, the pain running through me and the loss of Magnus - the love of my old soul still deep in my heart. At least, it grew to something almost like love, but not quite anything as pure. Perhaps after this, I can rest.

We had a lot of fun in our time together. Naively, I thought it would stay that way forever.

He was...complicated, but had so much light in his heart, and he always smiled a lot. I am thankful for that; his smile, as now I find it hard to remember the small details. The love in his heart seemed to become more apparent to me, like a warm glow as time moved on. I glowed too.

The first time the light came, we were laughing together. It had been a night of learning for me, and time seemed to have gone very fast. When I awoke to find I was dead, I had no idea what time it was, and the night stayed dark. Magnus took pleasure in teaching me things, and what I could do surprised me.

I also realised that Magnus was not as serious as he first appeared to be. He was so much more. My new teacher made me accept my death, told me I had to accept it or I would turn bitter as each night fell upon me, casting me deeper into despair.

I did not want that. No, instead I wanted to be with him, to feed on the passion of his strong soul, to feel protected and warm in a place where I thought no warmth would come. And the things he taught me, well...

I found I could move so fast, it looked like I had vanished and turned up in a different spot of the room. This made me more than slightly dizzy at first, but I soon got used to it.

"Your memory has faded, has it not?" enquired

Magnus. He seemed to know exactly what I was going through and what I was to expect and he always seemed at least two steps again of me in expectation of my feelings.

"Yes, it has. I can remember fragments of what happened just before but..." I replied. He nodded in understanding.

"My memories lingered for a while, and then grew dim. I cannot remember much else than when I first awoke from death - apart from the things that were most valuable to me. "I have become accustomed to reading my journals, it is what connects me to my old life. In time you will become...comfortable with your past memories."

I knew he was right, I could feel myself becoming used to this already. I knew I had to ask him something.

"What about others, others who are dead the way we are?" I spoke up, slightly nervous of his reply. A laugh escaped from him, he couldn't help himself. It made me almost jump. He laughed and he laughed, as I watched him, perplexed at what I had said. At last he replied:

"Others! I wondered when you would come to ask such a question. They move so fast, they are everywhere. They do not like to be disturbed; I may as well be here alone! Not here in this room, but alone in this world. They are far too serious; in fact, I think some of them have gone insane. You must stay away from some of those creatures; they are kept here for a reason and they can be dangerous."

I laughed slightly with him, but a strange small feeling of dread slowly trickled into my heart. Magnus's humour confused me slightly, and I also began to wonder, what were we doing here?

As I started to feel this in its full intensity, I looked down at my body to see it slowly disappearing. Startled, I cried out, could this feeling be doing this to me? Was I going to the place I was meant to be? A feeling of dreadful loss poured into me, almost a crippling feeling that caused light 'cramps' all over my body, like butterflies.

"Don't worry," Magnus quickly said, "this happens when the sunlight comes. I will also fade when the intensity of the light hits me; I have been here for much longer than you so therefore am stronger, more rooted to this world."

Confused by his words, I felt myself grow faint, then; darkness. As I fell into the world of my unconscious, I watched Magnus's image blur.

Magnus had often told me about the next part, how many before me had come to offer him company, how many had failed to materialise or return back to him after the dawning period, as he later named it. How some spirits just seemed to... disappear. These thoughts entered his mind as he sat, drumming his fingers, watching the slow sunrise, before at last he started to fade.

Perhaps we are here only in darkness because we were in darkness when we died? Perhaps we are not meant for the sun, as we are dark souls or perhaps evil? I know the horror stories that ghosts only come out at night, but surely we are not simple ghosts?

I believed that tale was only because generally we as humans – mortals - are scared of the dark, and evil spirits can only spook us at that time. Black, the colour of evil. We are only scared of things we cannot see.

It was the next night when I came back into our world. I awoke, as it were, to find myself standing before him, in the same position I had been in before. I found myself stumbling slightly; as I looked into Magnus's eyes and saw the wonder he beheld me with. He was relieved, I could tell although he hid it well.

I smiled at him, remembering our last moments before the sun came up. I understood now, he was not as sensitive to the light as me, and therefore it took him slightly longer to fade. Standing before me now, he looked solid as ever before.

"I am glad to see you," he spoke first, "Many a time I have been left alone once more."

I shivered slightly at the thought of what had happened to me, and where others before me had gone.

"You are a strong spirit Night, I knew that when I first sensed you. Some of the souls simply...waver away like dust," he told me.

I certainly felt strong, especially with him. I couldn't quite work out how I was feeling towards him at the time, but I knew I did not want to be separated from him; this strong entity. Soon after that, we decided to venture into the night together.

The city was filled with streetlights and people, glowing faces everywhere. There was music playing, and it was a busy night. I was taken in with the scene, fascinated by everything around me I felt that overwhelming love I had felt the night before.

Magnus seemed to shy away from the light at first, as I preferred to dance in it. We watched people down below, but I did not pay much attention to them. They were nothing to me, compared to the two beings we were, racing around the sky.

Almost my entire attention was taken up by Magnus. The streetlights made me first shine bright, then translucent. I knew already I could not be seen by the living, and I felt great joy at being around them again even if only to observe.

They did not hold my attention for long, as everything I saw or touched seemed different. Perhaps new and brighter, more beautiful in my new, spirit eyes. It was all new to me in a way, although a lot of the things looked familiar, they were also startlingly different. It was like a new world. I wanted to take Magnus's hand and dance with him; I got so caught up in the movement of the city. I was momentarily amazed by it.

"I feel like I want to dance, my body in time with the movement of life," I told him, holding his hand I swung around in the sky. Instead of doing the same, he reached out to me and held me close. It felt amazing to be in his arms, completely weightless as we floated in the night sky. I took in everything in those few moments and finally I looked into his eyes and they were looking down at mine.

"You are amazing," he whispered, looking so captivated the light seemed to dart around his eyes, making them shine golden.

I could see the spirits now. They really were everywhere, but mostly moving so fast it was difficult to take them in. Bursts of white light, a brush of air, sometimes a face, eyes briefly meeting mine.

Later on that night, I saw something that truly terrified me. A girl, thin and straggly, she looked truly depressed and ill. I saw her walking along the street, although her feet did not move and she was slightly above the pavement. Her long blonde hair blew behind her like long ropes, her face so dull and drawn. A couple were coming towards her, she moved right through them as if they were not there, invisible to her. She was one of us, I had known that straight away, and as I slowly decided to float down to confront her, the gentle hand of Magnus held me back.

"No," he told me.

I felt a certain amount of loss resonating from this girl. I couldn't quite place how I felt this, but she was carrying it around deep in her heart. She was wearing old ripped jeans and a frayed light pink top, baggy on her thin body. She walked with her head down, in a kind of slump.

"Stay away from ones like that, they can try to harm you," Magnus told me. I turned to look at him, his face now an expression of sorrow.

"Why?" I asked him.

"They are weak souls, lost you could say. Some of them will try and tear you down. After a while I don't think some of them are in a proper state of mind. I sometimes ponder that their souls have retired deep inside them, and they automatically just walk, like that." Magnus spoke quietly, with respect for these souls. I squeezed his hand.

Shocked by this horrible thing, and that it was now part of 'our world', I couldn't bring myself to say anything. It felt wrong, very wrong.

We went back in silence, my fascination still on all the things around me. Magnus explained that there were a lot of souls like the girl we had seen, and he had sometimes thought that perhaps we were in a kind of limbo. What happened to me was very unfair he told me, it was not my time to die. He told me he saw it happen, that my throat had been slit by an intruder. I had been murdered.

Being told this by Magnus brought back my fragmented memory that flashed before my eyes, the feeling of panic and the awful truths that came with it. The pain came back to me and I remembered the dark figure I could not quite see.

I remembered a hint of a struggle, glass being knocked over. For a time I cried loudly when I remembered this, cried out violently for what I once had been; the beautiful young girl that had only begun a career in journalism, settling down after many travels to the wildernesses of the world around me. I cried out because of the terrible unfairness, the sense of loss I have for my life and what I couldn't even remember.

I could not see myself in the mirror, although sometimes if I was feeling strong enough, I could see a very light reflection of myself in a window. I do not know how this came to be, I have no answers. I sometimes think that by time, I grew stronger, which made me remember Magnus's words about not fading so easily in the light. But he always seemed so strong to me, like a pillar, or my anchor to the world.

Chapter Five

I met Mandi outside the entrance to the hostel; he was dressed much smarter than earlier, but still possessed an easy, casual air about him, his brilliant smile shining through.

I smiled back and together we walked down the beach, the sun already starting to recede as we walked towards it. It was a beautiful night, and a beautiful place that he had chosen for us to dine although really, food wasn't at the top of my agenda.

I think he noticed my change from earlier, sensed a feeling of excitement that welled up inside me; yet this was not down to him, as he would soon find out. The restaurant was decorated by red hanging lanterns, and as we sat at one of the outside tables I immediately told him of my plan.

"I want to go to one of the islands," I said, looking full of confidence and ease, so sure of myself. He looked at me, astonished he laughed.

"Night…you want me to show you the islands? Well that is no problem, we can take a boat tomorrow," he replied as his cocktail arrived on cue. He took a sip, savouring it.

"No, I want you to take me there and then I want to be alone…to stay there, just for a day or two," I said as I watched his reaction cautiously. He almost choked.

"Oh no, no, no, no, no! Just leave you there, on an island, girl, I cannot let you do that!"

"Please, I need this," I looked at him, searching for some sort of recognition in his eyes. He mirrored my gaze, seeming to find a sort of understanding in my eyes. He relaxed back in his chair, seeming to think for a few moments. We sat in silence.

"Okay, okay… you know there are some nice places you might be able to stay at on some of the larger islands-

"No," I interrupted, "I want to stay on one of the small islands, where I can be alone, just for a couple of days. Let me do this."

"But...can I ask why?" It was not the response I expected from him, and I hesitated. Did I even know why myself?

"I just have to...get away, sort my head out. That's all I ask," I told him this sincerely. He seemed to ponder on my words, looking slightly uncomfortable before finishing off his pina colada.

"I'll see what I can do, I might know of a place," he spoke more softly now, his voice less vibrant, he continued with, "I can tell you are a wild spirit. Man, we haven't even ordered dinner yet!"

"This is serious Mandi...do you ever think you're here for a reason? Well...I think I'm lost. Truly lost, and I need to try and find who I was again, and work out who I am now," I told him with as much difficulty as I could have made for myself.

"You're the same person Night, you should know that. Your soul is always there with you, and I can tell you it is beautiful," he looked at me sincerely, and I stared back, shocked but quickly brushing off his words.

"Look, are you going to take me to this island or not?"

He laughed, and nodded that he would. On one condition; that he could borrow his brother's boat for the day. He'd never wanted to be a fisherman, he told me, because of his father so he instead became a guide. He knew everything about the local area and loved the land that he was born on, returning to it after some years of travelling in Europe.

I felt so grateful for Mandi's understanding that night; we talked for hours and I told him what I'd held back earlier in the bar, why I felt the way I did. Like I had some sort of traveller's curse or something. His face darkened.

"Do not joke about curses...just be glad that none have been placed upon your soul," he told me in a strange sort of voice.

It momentarily halted the conversation and for the first time that night I felt a chill sweep over my bare arms. I dazedly touched my skin and felt goose bumps. I laughed, shakily.

"Okay," I said, "so what's the plan for tomorrow?"

"You gather your things and we leave early, around six. You keep this quiet and tell no-one, got it?"

I nodded, as he seemed deadly serious.

"And Night...please promise me you'll take good care of yourself," he told me. I smiled, and left the restaurant to walk back towards the beach. I felt invigorated, energised at the prospect of two days in absolute paradise. I followed my instinct and ran towards the sea, feeling the cool water rush over my feet and splash up onto my legs.

I looked up at the stars shining so brightly and clearly in the sky, and felt what could be happiness; I'd forgotten what it felt like. It was a beautiful thing to behold, the stars staring down at me, this tiny speck in a universe full of things I could never see or imagine.

I felt an inner strength I had not felt in a long time, as if I could start swimming and go on for miles until I finally collapsed on the shores of...somewhere. The islands were pulling me, although I didn't know why. Now, I wish I had never gone there.

After a couple of minutes I heard a splash behind me and looked back to see Mandi. Smiling he came towards me, lifted me up and ran deeper into the sea before dropping me in the water. I screamed and splashed him although by then we were both soaking wet and laughing like kids.

I slept well that night, a dreamless sleep that pulled me deep under like a dark blanket covering my consciousness.

It seemed like only seconds had passed since my head hit the pillow when I awoke to the light creeping through my window. It was early yet I felt rested and secure inside my warm bed. Yawning and stepping out onto the wooden floor I looked out the window, to see the beginnings of the day.

Five minutes to six and I was packed and leaving the room, unable to contain my excitement. Mandi had managed to borrow his brother's boat and he had told me exactly what island we would be heading to; it was one of the smallest islands, isolated and safe from other tourists, hopefully for the time during my stay.

Not many people scattered the beach as I ran down to meet Mandi, the sand immediately getting into my sandals, the beginnings of the bright sun greeting me. He was there waiting, with the small boat and some bottled water. He waved to me as I neared the shore.

"Are you sure you want to do this?" He asked me, looking bright and well-prepared for the journey, his skin taking on an almost luminous glow in the morning sun. I smiled.

"Absolutely! Let's go!"

So we set off into the sea, the waves around us mild as I looked across to the islands, trying to figure out which of them we were headed to. They didn't look that far off and I knew that I would be able to find peace within myself if only given the space. I had brought my digital camera and one of my small leather-bound books so I could keep a journal of my time alone on the island.

As it started to get warmer, I felt the sun on my skin making me hot; I could feel beads of sweat running down my forehead. Mandi's attention was always on the sea ahead, although there were few boats out in the sea; fisherman, mostly.

It seemed a long time that we travelled over the water, and each island got more remote until finally Mandi pointed at the one we were visiting; it looked perfect, isolated. My own little paradise.

I felt absolutely no fear, no sense of reproach from that island, not then. I still wonder why I was so determined to be alone, to stay somewhere so far from the normal tourist trails but then I always was one looking for adventure.

Perhaps my soul was fragile and taking it somewhere so remote could only feed that fragility. Either way, I do not dwell on my mistakes, even if now that is all I have to occupy myself with. It is a dark trap, one I try to stay away from, yet I must recount this tale once more with all the art my little wordsmith soul can manage; for my sake, not yours dear reader – whoever you are.

And so we reached the island with no worries or trauma whatsoever. The water stayed a wonderfully clear, blue aqua colour and no would-be killer sharks approached the small wooden boat that belonged to Mandi's brother.

Mandi, on the other hand grew less cheerful the closer we got to the island that he would soon leave me on. I could tell that he was not convinced by my strong determination to isolate myself; he was perhaps even worried about me. But there was something else, something he was keeping from me that I just could not figure out.

He was wearing a blue shirt and patterned shorts which suited his bright personality, yet his gaze into the horizon did not suit the Mandi that I so briefly knew. Although I registered these thoughts and feelings, he did not try to talk me out of going, not once.

Perhaps he knew a lost cause when he saw it, or perhaps he just respected my wishes and let me keep my business to myself; he was just that sort of guy.

When I first set foot on the island that had beckoned me, I felt the slightest, almost undetectable sense of unease that I quickly pushed to the back of my mind as I accepted the bottled water and food supplies from Mandi.

Looking around the beach was generally quite small, with large plants and vegetation leading into the centre of the island. It was bigger than I'd first thought, and looking into the darkness that dwelled there I wondered how long the island usually went uninhabited, at least by the tourist trap.

Mandi stayed with me for a small while, making sure the boat was fit to travel the waters and taking a well deserved rest. As he began to ready the boat again, he sighed.

"I can't believe I am letting you do this," he told me, again arousing my suspicions.

"Well, why are you?" I ask him, eyebrow raised. He looked at me, hard this time.

"I can tell you can take care of yourself," he replied, "just watch out while you're here, I can't let anything bad happen to you."

I thought this was an unusual thing to say, but held back my words as I lingered over our goodbye.

He said one last thing to me as we stood there together, awkwardly on the beach.

"Night," he said as he looked seriously into my eyes, taking me back a little he continued, "I can sense there is a darkness in you. It is strong, and you battle with it, no? Don't let it win."

As his words lingered in my mind, I knew this was the last I'd see of Mandi for two days now. I looked over to the neighbouring islands, the sight of which drew a slight sense of ease for me to see that I was not so far from civilisation; I saw movement across the waters on the one of the opposing beaches.

So I sat on the pure white sands and watched Mandi sail away, the small, battered white boat gradually turning into a tiny white speck in the distance. I sat and watched it disappear for as long as it took, and then finally stood up and took a look at my new surroundings, taking everything in as if for the first time.

I registered some small pebbles, some larger pebbles, a marker tree and an old rope. Apart from that, the trees and plants looked thick and heavy – perfect shade. I wandered the island registering all its little markers, occasionally taking my digital camera from my pocket and snapping at everything from the wildlife to the beautiful beach and the waves that were now crashing against the shore. After a while, I found the perfect sitting rock, and pondered on my new-found situation.

Even though I'd been waiting for this moment for quite a while, a feeling of dread now trickled into my mind – now I had to face up to my problems, I had absolutely no excuses.

I fetched my exercise book and trusty pen, deciding to sit under the shade of the marker tree and write down some of my feelings, perhaps even to enter into my travel diary when I returned to the hostel. Somehow it seemed important to write everything down.

Time past quickly as I wrote down my innermost thoughts and feelings, yet images of the darkness behind me kept creeping into my mind, which disturbed me slightly. I had been doodling a large sun on the notepad when finally I set the book down and looked up into the sky, soon dozing off into a deep sleep.

For some unknown reason, I dreamt of the old man that I thought I'd glimpsed back at the hostel. I dreamt of his rotten looking eyes, aged skin and dry lips, paint on his forehead and cheek coloured blue and red. In the dream the sky was starting to darken, a deep red smear across the landscape as if someone had smudged blood across the blue.

I wanted to ask him who he was, or why he was there yet I couldn't open my mouth. I wasn't in the least bit terrified, but his face...looked somehow very wrong to me. The sense of dread I'd felt when I set foot on the island returned; only now it was ten times worse and fear filled my heart. The irrational thought entered my mind that perhaps he was trying to warn me.

I felt his old fingers stroke my back, making me shiver and prayed to be brought out of this nightmare, the smell of his breath foul and ancient. It was then I woke up.

I opened my eyes to the same view, darkening skies filled with red and his fingers were still running down my back. I swiftly turned around to see nothing, just my exercise book which was blowing open in the breeze.

I spent the rest of the night unleashing my wild side, walking through the darkness of the island feeling the thick rubbery feel of the giant leaves against my bare skin. I wore nothing but a sheer white caftan that barely covered the start of my legs. The breeze was cool and welcoming against the hot air, and I breathed in the smell of the heavy plant life, feeling as if I was the only one in the world. I heard the odd noise of animals in the undergrowth of course, insects and flies, maybe a few small frogs. Nothing more; there were no humans on the island apart from myself.

After the exploration I ran onto the beach and threw myself into the dark water in a way that I hadn't really allowed myself to do back on the mainland. I completely immersed myself in it; not even knowing which way was up or down, savouring the cold water on my smooth skin, only surfacing to breathe in the cool night air in hungry gasps that filled my lungs with comfort and life.

I realised without a care in the world that my feet could no longer touch the bottom of the sands, and I treaded water while taking in the wonderful feeling of being complete. My heart beat fast in my chest, making me feel more alive than I'd ever felt in my life and I was thankful for everything I'd had to give.

It was a beautiful night and after so long I think I finally found what I was looking for. I stared into the darkness for a long time, not wanting to give up the water and head back to the beach. In that darkness I think I managed to mend my soul. I saw that it was stunning and once again I found love; this time for myself.

Chapter Six

Magnus gradually taught me everything I needed to know, his words forever etched in my soul. My teacher, my love; he seemed so strong to me, always. Sometimes I remember his presence as if he was still in the room with me, although I know deep down that he has gone, departed from me.

To think he would watch me sends a chill down my spine, and I wonder exactly what has become of him, spirited away by the ghostly haloed lights.

As the nights passed by I learned little about my master – that was the way I thought of him, pathetic as that may seem; I was in a dark place. He'd never wanted to be such a thing, but without him I knew I was weak.

As I appeared that night once again to the sight of my new found love, my new fascination, I saw the vaguest of smiles on his sober face, his eyes bright as ever with just a hint of a curl hanging down. His hair had been almost shoulder-length when he'd died - something that has now become popular again in the world of the living. He was, in a sense, in fashion, which displeased him eternally.

The night was perfectly calm with no wind and clear skies. As I looked through the window once again I subconsciously searched for the lights but saw nothing. Magnus noticed me looking.

"If you are looking for God, I think you will be severely disappointed," he words seemed to wake me from my daze, and only then did I realise what I had been looking for. I smiled briefly, shaking my head.

He moved towards a lit candle on the table of the old attic, and swiftly blew it out, throwing me a quick glance to see that I was watching him. Transfixed, I watched him touching the dust that lay there, seemingly displeased with the level that had gathered over the years. I wanted to learn how to touch, and said so.

"I want you to teach me everything you know," I said, confident enough to voice my burning desire to learn. He turned to me once more, looking deadly serious.

"And indeed I will teach you, follow me," he replied, and with such a swiftness I was not ready for, left through the window pane and through the night skies. I followed, still unsure of not breaking the glass, but managed nevertheless to slip through it as if it had never been there.

He headed towards a small church, surrounded by fields and little light to guide me. It did not matter, for I sensed his presence in a way I could not have done when I first passed over to the dark.

In the narrow, dusty windows of the church I saw the faintest of lights and realised that candles had been lit inside. Magnus was now also inside the building, waiting for me.

I hesitated at the door, unsure that a spirit could enter a church – places that were supposed to be holy, houses of God. Cautiously I put my hand over the wood, although I could not feel its substance. I let myself enter, greeted by the sight of Magnus looking deeply impatient yet also warm with the glows of the candles that were set up behind the altar.

The pews were dark, and as I moved forward I was surprised to see an elderly woman sitting alone in a black woollen shawl and hat. I realised soon after that she was a spirit, although she didn't so much as register our presence and instead shivered, muttering under her breath.

Magnus beckoned me forward, and I looked questioningly into his eyes.

"Why have you brought me here?" I asked.

"For you to see for yourself; it is a church – nothing more. You wanted to learn, didn't you?" He responded, nonchalantly. I nodded while looking around, silent for a moment.

"Look," he said, picking up an old dusty copy of the bible, "it can't hurt you. It's just a book. Would you like to try?"

"Will you teach me how to touch it?" I asked, feeling confused at being brought to such a place.

"Of course," he said, an odd look forming in his eyes. I glanced once more at the old lady who sat looking miserly and confused, surrounded by the wooden panelling of the old church. Cobwebs and thick dust lurked in every corner and large beams hung from the low ceiling.

"This is her refuge, leave her be," Magnus told me, a note of firmness in his voice. He walked over to the candles, and used his force to blow upon them, making them quiver.

I slowly stepped towards the place he was standing, awaiting instruction.

"You have to focus your energy on the spot you want to make an impact on. You are still weak, but as time goes on and you linger in this world, with the right teaching your strength will grow."

"I see," I replied, trying to take this information in. However I couldn't figure out where my energy was centred, or how to activate it; I stared at the flickering candles quietly.

"It's all about balance," Magnus continued, "You have to find the strength within you and push it up inside, then expel it like this."

I watched as he traced his finger along the dust of the table, around the glass of the candle holders. I tried to touch the table but failed, and again. He watched, smiling faintly.

"Try the candles," he said.

I focused my attention on the candles, and tried to feel the energy deep down in my spiritual body. I could sense it there like a low fire, although how I did not know as it was not something I'd ever sensed before.

Coming close to the candles, I blew at them, making one of them flicker. I tried the same again, only more so and the furthest candle was extinguished.

Magnus clapped, looking pleased at my progress as a spiritual entity. Soon I was able to move the candles around the table, although each time I drew on my energy I felt myself getting weaker. Magnus assured me that his ease would come to me in time, but I was determined to lift one of the candles using my life force.

At first I could only pick up the glass holder a few centimetres before it fell back to the table, almost toppling over. He watched as I failed to give up, making more attempts to lift the glass between my fingertips, making the candle flicker from time to time until I eventually found my grasp. The candle floated mid-air until a noise from the pews startled me, making me drop the candle to the floor.

Immediately the small flame caught on the wooden flooring and Magnus had to act fast before the building burned to the ground. With a professional flair, he brought it quickly under control before turning sharply to the noise and the source of my amazement.

The old woman was now softly moaning to herself and I noticed she was staring at us, in a way that at once made me feel uncomfortable. Her hair was a thick grey, long and curly and on her badly aged finger she wore a gold ring consumed by a dark red ruby.

"She is harmless, do not be afraid," Magnus whispered as the spirit began to stand from the pew. She looked to be trembling under her shawl, her eyes looking glazed and confused. She started to murmur words that I could not understand at first, but then she spoke louder.

"What right do you think you have, coming to the house of the Lord? You are evil, curse thee! Get out, go on! Leave!" Her voice was cracked and deep, almost shaky.

I felt myself getting closer to Magnus as she approached us, but before he could do a thing she flew at us fast.

All I could see was her haunted eyes as she came past us, through us, her anger obvious on her wrinkled, pallid face. It was horrible, to see that her spirit was so obviously insane, knowing that there was nothing we could do to help her. As I felt her energy pass through me, the candles blew out sharply.

Then she was gone, and we were left alone in the darkness of the church. I turned to Magnus; I wanted to ask him why she had acted that way, if there was any way we could help…but no words came out.

He stood for a few seconds, head bowed to the ground before elegantly picking up the fallen candle and placing it back upon the table. House-keeping done, he turned to look at me, eyes alive and searching for my emotions; I was shaken up and he reached out to me, steadying me close to his energy I was able to draw from it.

But Magnus was unsympathetic, simply dismissing my shock at the insanity of the spirit that had 'attacked' us. He ordered me to come back to the table.

"Now, light them," he told me kindly yet firmly as I looked at him in surprise. Looking around the room I saw no matches or lighters to aid me. I turned to him, questioningly.

"Do it," his voice was sharper now, "use your mind!"

For a few seconds I was frozen in front of the candles, before I began my attempt at re-igniting them. At first, nothing came to me and I wondered how I could possibly set something alight using only my power.

"Concentrate, feel the energy growing warm inside of you. Can you feel it?" he was talking at me but his voice seemed far away as I focused intently on my centre. After a while, I began to feel a slight heat – I could imagine it as a dull light that glowed inside of me - that gradually built up and I followed his words, pushing it up further until I would be able to project it.

"Night, you have to keep hold of your power, do not let your emotions overcome you - you cannot let it get out of control; never that - it can be very dangerous," Magnus was raising his voice as he felt the heat around me grow, and I awaited his instruction.

"Now, focus it towards the candles but gradually, be careful!" He shouted as I finally let it go and seemingly out of nowhere the warmth took shape and fire moving forward towards the candles, burning the wax of most in the centre and turning it to liquid, while the others on the outside were successfully set alight.

Once it was out of me I feel suddenly weak, as if I was about to collapse or lose consciousness; unusual for a ghost.

Magnus was looking at me with an odd look on his face, and as he stepped towards me he reached out and I felt the warmth of his energy flood my spiritual body, cleansing me and replenishing me.

"Yes, that was exactly it!" He told me, "However, Night, you have to learn how to control this power. In death, your emotions can sometimes be explosive and if you do not harness the power of fire completely then it can be controlling and unpredictable for those involved. Not many of us learn how to possess this power, so you have done very well on this night."

I felt almost unable to speak as his words sank into me, I knew now that if I were to properly learn this power it would also take a lot of strength; something my spirit was not used to.

"It has sapped your energy, hasn't it? I can tell, I know what it is like," Magnus continued. I turned to him, incredulous.

"I don't trust it, Magnus," I replied, his face turning on me with all the intensity of his will, "There is so much I feel, how can I tell what is real and how do I control this…thing? What if it becomes the controlling one...you're scaring me."

"Come on," Magnus said, "I think you've learned enough for now."

It was one of the last lessons he taught me, the answers to my questions were left unanswered.

Chapter Seven

Magnus often spent a lot of time dwelling in the attic of an old house. A lot of his possessions were stored there, although I never asked him how that had come to be. He took me there and I felt a sort of warmth, surrounded by his writings and books, his inkwells and pens. Belongings were scattered in boxes around the old wooden floors.

I remember him sitting at his antique wooden desk, head in his hands, thinking. Now it comes to mind, he was always a bit of a tormented soul, but always so loving, so very deep in his thoughts and emotions.

The first time he took me there I realised the place was just as much his as the people who owned it. He explained to me his presence there was never noticed, as the attic had been left entirely alone for many years. I could tell he had spent a lot of time alone there as the years had passed – it just seemed to resonate his personality, something that is probably very hard for a ghost to achieve.

I always wondered why he chose me to spend his time with. I had a feeling that he was intrigued by me, after or because he had seen my death. Perhaps he fell in love with me even then. I could not appreciate the value of his gesture towards me at the time, but now I understand that it is uncommon for a spirit to make such a union with another soul.

The attic was the place we always returned to - safe - our hiding shelter from the world. No other spirits seemed to pass by whilst we were there. Perhaps they knew to stay away from us.

We ventured out together most nights. I knew Magnus was always looking over me - I felt that he was my protector, always there to see my mistakes and discoveries. I knew he was stronger than me, much stronger. I remember it was one of those nights I discovered we could draw energy from the living, in short bursts sort of like the recharging of a battery.

"Try it, it will bring them no harm," he had said to me, as I looked down on the people walking through the street. I singled out a young girl, vibrant and pretty. She had very long hair, shining brightly in the light. I found myself sweeping down so I was right next to her, able to draw the energy out. With my entire mind I focused and for a while I was shrouded in brightness, my spirit absorbing this light. It made me feel power for a short while, and it also gave me an unusual feeling of pleasure.

The city looked so vibrant and I looked up to Magnus who was smiling down at me, his skin stood out so pure and white. Everything looked even more beautiful; it had given me a buzz.

I suppose I had found a kind of happiness there with him, observing and taking in everything that I could possibly learn about the world. I re-visited some of the places I had travelled to in my past, feeding my memories and looking at the sights with my new eyes, making everything feel so much more vibrant in the night. We visited places I'd longed to see, unable to do so in my life as a broke traveller/journalist, writing stories and earning just enough to scrape by. I saw things I'd only ever dreamed about in life, although it saddened me that I could not look upon these sights in the light.

It must have been a couple of weeks later when he first left me. I 'awoke' as it were, to find myself staring at the now accustomed sight of Magnus, his tall figure with the beautiful dark curls that perfectly accompanied his pale skin, the lightest of marks on his left cheek. I realised then that he was my only companion in this world. I felt myself frowning, as he was gathering up some of his things.

"Magnus?" I asked, questioningly. He turned to me.

"Now do not fear, I have something I have to take care of. I promise I will not be long, Sweet." He told me, his voice cool and calm, his eyes bright, his look was one of caring.

"You're leaving me here?" I felt such an unwelcome, unexpected dread of being left alone so suddenly.

"I will return soon. Please, read my journals, I'd like you to learn about my past life." I glanced at the big wooden desk stacked with old leather bound books and stray bits of browned paper; he had never offered to share this with me before. He gave me one last smile, and then left as if he had never been standing before me.

Well, what was I to do? I felt totally lost without him and that was no doubt a warning signal; the warmth I felt from him being near was quickly pulled away in the same fashion as a blanket. I shivered slightly, although this was a trick as I could not feel the cold any longer.

I did as I was told, of course. I began to read his journals, and discovered so much more about my companion that I was in the end, glad to know. He had always been a bit of a loner, a traveller just like I had once been.

I was amazed at the many travels he had been on, to so many distant sounding lands. I became absorbed in Magnus; the man, the wanderer, the brave, somewhat arrogant soul that had spent time over these journals. In fact, I became so transfixed by his work, I had read almost six of them by the time I realised he had not yet returned to me. Worry started to creep in through the cracks of the emotional barrier I'd erected in his presence, and once more I wished for knowledge of his whereabouts.

I was surprised to find that Magnus had married, his bride being ten years younger than himself. He had married at the age of twenty eight, not long before his journals of travel had finished. I slowly put the book down. Why did it upset me to think of him in this way? There was no doubt regarding his love for her, as he spoke of her with only the utmost affection. Her name had been Viola.

An entry from Magnus's Journal:

As I sit here alone on the loud, infernal machine I wonder once again why I am here and not at home with the people who are close to me. Viola will of course have her company, and the farm will go on as usual but I am left with a sorrow in my heart, as if it is twisting under the strain of being pulled in different directions. My Viola, why can't I stay with you?

Instead, I chose to subject myself to my darkest feelings and intuitions, never able to break free into the light. When I am with you, I feel I cannot be with you and when I am far from you, all I want is to hold you in my arms.

But there is nothing I would not do to make you happy, and you are not happy. My only wish is for you to read this and try to understand the situation I place myself in, even though it causes me terrible agony there is no way to escape it, my love.

My child you are too young to understand...

I put the book down and stared blankly at the wall. As I have said, time here does not mean the same to us as it does to you. I have no idea how long I spent trying not to agitate myself and doing it anyway. It seemed the more time I spent trying to occupy myself, the more time I spent simply in a state of unrest. Night turned to day and time after time I faded, with a wish to find him in front of me when I returned. There was nothing, I was met with nothing until I began to torture myself with thoughts.

All I could think of were those lonely, isolated thoughts that had gone through my head alone in Bangkok, alone on the island, alone in my London apartment; it was all too familiar. Perhaps I had been put on earth to learn a valuable lesson about loneliness, at least that's what it felt like. Going insane was not going to help matters however, so when the doorknob of the attic starting to open, I found it to be a worthy distraction.

It turned out to be a rather small but delightful looking young boy, maybe about ten or eleven years of age. He felt around for a light switch, and as his eyes adjusted to the light, he stared right at me. I of course, knew that this could not be true, but it caused a surge of panic inside me for just a moment, before his eyes moved to another spot in the room. He had looked through me, but not at all at me; was it just another dusty, empty room to the child's eyes.

I watched him as he picked up dusty old clothes, put them down again. Skimmed over the books, kicked an old can and then gingerly started to rifle through an old box of clothes and trinkets. He did not look like he was meant to be there, as the expression on his face was rather a guilty one. Watching this boy, I realised I should probably do something to keep him out – away from Magnus's things. But I didn't know how.

It was like watching a small innocent spider creep across the room, and my fascination grew as I admired his shiny chestnut brown hair and cornflower blue eyes. I realised I would never be able to have one of those little cretins now... No, I'd passed up that chance long ago – my own fault. It gave me a dull ache deep down in my very soul and I pushed the rogue thought out of my mind.

I was partly relieved when he left, as Magnus probably wouldn't take kindly to this visitor. What to do, I thought. If it was possible to start tearing my hair out, I probably would have started already.

Magnus finally returned to me a day later, and soon it was as if he had never left me alone in that room. He put his things down upon the table, and I wondered if it was really him. He smiled at me, showing that his business was apparently taken care of.

"I missed you," he told me, arm touching mine. I looked up into his eyes, and they stared back at me so openly, it struck me that he had nothing to hide.

"Where have you been?" I asked him, questioningly.

"I'll tell you some day," he answered me, "but really, it's just something I have to do every so often. It certainly cleared my mind anyway." I looked at him with raised eyebrows. He certainly seemed at peace. I did not, could not own this creature, and I felt so relieved just to be in his company again that I dared not to question it further. I smiled at him, our energies starting to synchronise as we sat together, surrounded by the dust. The stars shone in the night sky, and I felt myself content in his presence.

After that, things went back to normal in that we spent every moment enjoying each other. He showed me ways in which our spirits could be intimate, and I could read his innermost thoughts, at least the ones he wanted me to see. It was as if our minds, our spirits temporarily melted together although of course it wasn't a physical reaction, more an unknown one.

I was surprised at how our energies started reacting to each other, but pleasantly. I could not have imagined feeling these feelings with anyone, so strange and alien they seemed to be. We were so intense, and yet we had so much fun together. And yet always, in between everything were his occasional visits to somewhere completely beyond my perception. It was the only thing he kept hidden from me, and slowly it made me want to know more.

Magnus was a strong spirit, and I had no right to demand to know everything about him. I felt certain possessiveness however, and it only worried me further. Every time he left, I felt utterly helpless to try and stop him. I was left alone with my thoughts, our union severed with barely a trace of him.

I watched the living more and more during these bouts of loneliness and soon became fascinated by their innocence, their carelessness and their enjoyment of life. Their frailty inspired in me wonder, and an immense love and respect for life. How easily their light could dim into darkness, and would they have any idea of what was to come next? It made me wonder if there was a next stage, if I was in-between worlds. I was simply a lost spirit, an observer, I supposed. I had no better idea than they did.

A young man with smooth, pale skin and brown hair, dressed smartly in a suit and carrying a briefcase; a young mother and daughter, both dressed in expensive clothes stepping into their upmarket people-carrier; an older gentleman, probably walking home to see his wife. None of them knew of what awaited them in death, or when that time would come. I sat and watched these people and wondered.

I began to hatch a plan; I simply had to follow Magnus as I could not bear not to know this secret! This would of course violate our trust, but it was slowly becoming painful for me to let him go like this and what if one day he never came back?

How would I have any idea what had happened to him, where to look? Maybe I was being childish, but I had to find out.

I knew I was behaving like a jealous mortal fool. However there seemed to be nothing I could do to stop this chain of thoughts. When Magnus returned to me, he always seemed slightly melancholy. He was always pleasant however, and he never really left for long. Silly really, I could not expect us to be joined at the proverbial hip. It was such a small thing.

And then it was the start of another beautiful, clear night when Magnus began to prepare himself for leaving. He always took with him a journal, hidden inside his coat. This puzzled me very much, where could he possibly be going that he was going to require his memories? I had stopped reading his journals, as that was not part of the creature that was with me now.

I acted coldly towards him, as he once again told me he must go. He touched my shoulder, as I continued to stare out of the open window. I watched him leave me.

It was not hard to follow Magnus. He was very much lost in thought, so much so that it surprised me and although he moved rather fast, it was obvious to me he was not so aware of the things around him. He always seemed in a slight daze when he returned, somewhat detached from what I was used to.

We were now somewhere in France, although I could not really keep track of where we were headed. It took much of my concentration just to keep track of him. His entity did not stay solid, moving at such speeds. It was more like a kind of energy trail, and I have no doubt in my mind if he wanted to lose me, he could do so with much ease. As far as I knew, he was not aware of my following him.

I could see below me now, small villages surrounded by hills. We had passed the larger cities and were somewhere in the south, moving more slowly now. I decided to stop completely, to watch him from afar. I felt a considerable amount of unease, confusion and a large sense of guilt. Did I really have to know?

Halfway up a hill, he stopped to look down on a small and simple cottage. It was occupied by a very elderly woman. Magnus watched her, and I watched Magnus as this old lady proceeded to feed her hens. I could see she had lit a fire inside her house, and she was boiling water in a small kettle above it. It was one of the loneliest places I had ever seen, and all I could hear was the wind blowing.

Magnus was now standing on the ground, watching the elderly woman with a strange expression that I could barely make out on his face. Who was this woman?

"And I knew that I would never leave her," Magnus spoke, reading from his journal, "my love for her will never be tainted, and she has my utter devotion for the rest of time. My Viola. Not even my adventures could keep me away from you any longer." He looked down, a sad expression on his face.

So this was his wife! I felt so much anger inside me, boiling like something I had never felt before. I felt like I had been betrayed, that this woman did no longer deserve to live and I wanted to destroy her and her simple little house, reduce it to ashes! How dare she take his attention like this, after all this time! He had moved on, why should he want to return here to this senile old woman instead of loving me?!

These thoughts of course, were completely irrational but I could hold this in no longer. I felt myself propelled forward; anger rising inside me higher and higher and he must have felt it then, as he looked up in fear. The woman was inside now, and I focused all my anger on this silly little house.

"No! No Night you must not! Leave her be!" Magnus shouted with rage, his voice filtered out by the wind around me. It felt like a small hurricane, all I could concentrate on was my anger.

The house suddenly exploded into large bright flames. It frightened me, it was like I had directed all my anger towards this house, or dare I say it, this woman and simply let it go. I watched it burn, the wind falling away now leaving the smell of burning.

Magnus was thrusting forward into the flames, backing out then circling the house. He was screaming out his torment, and never had I heard anything so awful. He looked so helpless, and I knew there was nothing he could do to save her now.

Already the house was falling apart, and all I could feel was sadness. I had no idea what had come over me, and I watched Magnus now in utter despair. I realised not even the hens would be spared.

His wife was gone. Would she linger? I really had no idea. It pained me to watch Magnus, the hurt he was feeling. He sat now, watching the house burn to ashes. He ignored me, lost completely in his own hurt, his own thoughts. I felt incredibly small as I floated there in the sky, watching him. All my anger had washed out of me and I felt much less as a being, most of my energy put into the flames.

The village had begun to stir now as someone had noticed the fire and raised the alarm. People were beginning to climb the hill.

The realisation sunk in that I had killed a living person. I had ended her life. A frail old lady of all the choices I could have made. The fascination I had with the living had somehow turned so easily into hate for Viola, an innocent. If I could have cried right then, I would have sobbed until my heart had burst. But I did not. Instead I watched him, as he sat there in silence.

I started to move, and then hesitated. He glimpsed the movement out of the corner of his eye. Suddenly, in a flash he was there, anger glowing like darts in his eyes.

"How DARE you! Look what you have done!" His words were so loud and full of hatred, they terrified me. I remained mute, stunned into silence.

"You followed me! You could not bear to let me be alone?! Well, consider yourself alone from now on," he spoke with such contempt, it hurt me deeply. Everything was summed up in the sneer he gave me. I could tell he was furious. All of a sudden he was gone, and I was left staring at the remains of an innocent little house alone in the hills.

After a while I returned to the attic room, to find it completely empty. There was a chill in my heart as I listened to the silence and for some time after I felt I had to punish myself. All I could think about was what I'd done, and the smell of burning haunted my thoughts. I have no idea how long I waited for him to return.

I found myself looking out the window, into the night. I searched for lights again, and for the first time I think I saw what I was meant to see. I began to think that maybe Magnus would never return; perhaps I should give up tormenting myself.

It was the same night when I sat at his desk, reading his journals for the last time. I felt a sudden rush of air, a change in the room and turned sharply towards the window. There he was, Magnus, looking in at me.

The haunted look on his face hurt me; I remembered all too well what I must have done to him. His face was pale like marble. Without a change in expression, he materialised through the walls. I stood up quickly, swiftly moving away from him I became suddenly frightened. I couldn't utter a word.

"Don't worry, I do not want to harm you," he spoke so calmly to me, and now he looked peaceful. He managed a sorrowful smile.

"I'm so sorry," I whispered, my pain for him overwhelming me all at once. I looked into his eyes, piercing green and saw serenity. He was back now, I felt so relieved he hadn't left me for good. Relief and sorrow, pain and happiness, the feelings flooded me entirely; how I had missed him so. I think he read my mind, as he came closer to me now, his hand reaching close to my face I could feel his warmth, our energies slightly meshing.

"I cannot stay here anymore darling; there is no need for me to stay. Can't you see that?" He sounded so serious. A dreadful feeling came over me and I couldn't understand how he could leave me now.

"No..." Once I had uttered the word, I knew it was true. There was nothing I could do to stop him.

"I have to go now," he spoke softly now, "I have found the way. So should you... you need the courage to face what you think it waiting for you on the other side. I loved you, remember that I loved you." He looked so beautiful, but where he was talking about going scared me. I wanted to say more to him, a proper goodbye but the way he looked at me, I knew he understood. I watched as he turned, and left through the glass in the window. I knew in my heart he had to leave now, his only tie to this earth had been severed and he should now be at peace.

I tried to ignore his last haunting words to me, but it made me sad to forget the things that had once meant a lot to me.

I slowly brought myself forward towards the pane, and watched as he floated into glowing light in the sky, and was gone. A beautiful angel had joined the skies.

Chapter Eight

I found myself encased in a deep, thoughtful loneliness; a solitary prison that only I could know. I slipped deeper and deeper into the realms of despair, unable to see myself the way I'd looked at so many lonely, lost souls, tortured and lost forever in time.

My time with Magnus kept playing over and over in my memory, as I remembered the terrible things that I had done; I had destroyed him, it was me that sent him away...and I only had myself to blame.

Amongst the litany of emotions that ran through my mind came anger. I was angry at myself and I thought then that I was truly alone. If there had ever been a God, how would he have let me kill someone so innocent. If there was a god, and if I was an angel, how could this have happened to me, what gave me these powers? They couldn't have come from heaven, but more like hell.

Was this a punishment from something I'd done in life? I couldn't even consider that possiblity... to face a fear that was overwhelming if I let it be.

Talking of hell, I was stuck in my own personal version and all I could do was dwell on Magnus's face, the hatred in his eyes, the anger in his voice; over and over again. I don't know what eventually pulled me away from insanity but somehow I was rescued.

I tried to keep him with me in my thoughts, his dark beauty, the man who'd once been strong and in death never aged a day over thirty. He'd been the one soul I'd ever really connected with, and now I was left with nothing.

Pain consumed me as I thought of all that had been taken from me, what had I done to deserve such cruelty? Even though my heart had died long ago I still felt every emotion sevenfold, clinging on to it like it was my last hope when I'd already given up.

As I cocooned myself in the small attic room, scared to let go of my thoughts, scared of losing the only part of him I really had left, I waited for each sunrise, for a release from the darkness.

But each time it was over I found myself back in that room; in the same darkness I wished so much to escape from. I even found myself praying to God as a last-ditch attempt to be free, but I was met with silence. As I looked out the window at the stars in the sky, still I saw no lights. There was nothing to give me hope.

But then I realised that really, I was free. I was free to roam wherever I chose, not to be locked inside this small, stuffy room for eternity. I could travel the world, or see those whom I'd once loved.

And then finally, my mind was also free; not chained to a memory of Magnus or to wallow in misery until I went as mad as some of the souls I'd witnessed by his side. I began to think, who was I before Magnus?

So instead of waiting for an eternity, I began to remember parts of my old life. All my old mistakes and heartache came back to me, filled me up inside. Parts of me wanted to cry as I thought of all the love I'd carried in my heart, all the fear and the times I spent under the beautiful golden suns that I'd never see again. I thought of old friends, family and the people I'd left behind when my life had been savagely taken from me. And the things I had done to tear out the love inside of me.

It was then that my thoughts started to centre again on the island. It had been in Satun, at the time when I'd decided to turn my life around. I had been happy then, a warm comfort that I'd managed to reach down and grasp from inside me.

Back then I'd thought everything was going to be okay, as I immersed myself in the cool waters and looked into the clear blue skies above. But then, it had all changed, hadn't it? The cool reality slowly sunk in as I sat there in his room. First it came in flashbacks; something I'd forgotten about swam underneath the memories like a dragon lurking beneath the surface, waiting to break through.

Why couldn't I remember? Perhaps my struggling soul had somehow managed to block out the memories, some things I just didn't want to remember. Or maybe we spirits forget about our lives when we pass through.

Think, I focused as I tried to force myself to remember, curled up in a barely there ball upon the floor of the small room that had somehow become like a second home.

At first all I remembered was the screams, but then slowly, gradually everything came flooding back to me as I silently digested all the old emotions and scenes that I had tried hard to block out when I had been alive.

It was my second day of perfect bliss in beautiful, remote isolation on the island. It was my island of hope, I thought to myself as I gathered some wood for the evening. I was determined to eat plenty that night, as so far a lot of the food that Mandi had left me stayed untouched. I reasoned with myself that it was probably the heat that had taken away my appetite.

It had so far been another calm day, the sun shining brightly down on me. I had taken shelter under my marker tree for most of the morning, just quietly contemplating what I would do when I returned to London.

It seemed ridiculous that I would be returning, after spending so long away from everything that I used to know. I found it hard to imagine walking down the busy streets and meeting friends who had wished me well all those months ago. It had seemed a lifetime ago that London had been my home.

Mandi would be returning for me in the morning, and I realised with a slight flutter in my stomach that I had missed him in spite of the short period we'd known each other. Laying the wood down next to my tiny version of a camp, I sat down and once again began to write.

I got a lot of writing done that afternoon, which proved to be not just a normal journal. I started to write fiction, something that I had always wanted to try but never really had the patience for, but now, under this tree with no distractions I found the story started to pour out of me as if being siphoned into my mind from somewhere magical…a place where stories originate perhaps.

Characters came alive and shone brightly in my mind like beautiful colours in a rainbow and litanies of words just seemed to spill from my mind. Their faces and actions echoed deep in my thoughts yet I needed no time to think about a plot; the words just came out and I kept writing without a question of how it was entering my mind.

My main character was deeply troubled yet beautiful in her own right, in a world consumed by madness and fury. She thought she was weak, when really there was nothing that she could not face, the strength within her shining through when faced with the difficult situation of loss and matters close to her own heart.

It was like nothing I had ever wrote before, and amazing myself I found the creativity to continue the story as if without a second thought, placing important events in the way of my character and another so that they longed to be together, yet were kept apart by forces out of their control. Until the end, that is.

Time passed quickly but I barely noticed, completely consumed in the story that seemed to take over every part of me. Not once did I notice the tide, or the sun starting to recede leaving a sunset I can only imagine would have been as beautiful as the night before, smears of orange and red lighting up the sky.

I only looked up when I found the pages were becoming more and more difficult to read, and noticed that it had become dark all around me. My stomach grumbled and I stood up to begin preparing my evening meal, leaving my book weighted down with a small but distinctive white rock.

Afterwards, when I was full and still sitting by the fire, contemplating the crashing waves on the shore I felt something unusual in the air that night. It was dark all around me, no lights in view for what seemed like miles, yet it felt like I was waiting for something to happen there.

Mandi would not be joining me again until morning, and I realised he was probably the reason I felt this way. It was then I decided to make the most of my last night on the island, and digging out my camera and flash I stood up to go for a wander in the darkness of the island's wilderness, determined to capture the harsh wilderness on film.

I felt a little wild in myself; I guess that's what isolation can do to you. I stepped carefully, a deliberate quietness in my movements as I felt my way through the island forest. I was surrounded by the sounds of the wildlife, and it gave me a little comfort knowing I was not alone. Feeling almost at one with it I started to capture the dark mood of the island with my camera.

After the first snap there was a rustle and then silence as the small animals and insects became aware of my presence, and with a cool confidence I took photo after photo of my beautiful, almost enchanting surroundings.

My favourite was of a beautiful, large silvery web that had been left by – excuse me - God knows how big a spider. Its different sections shone in the artificial light, capturing the dark fullness of the forest in all its glory.

I wandered in the forest for what seemed like hours, content in knowing that I was the only human inhabitant on the island; it made me feel safe. It might have been silly but I'd never been able to feel so at one with somewhere the way I did with this island – as if I could do whatever I wanted. It was my paradise, although when Mandi came for me I knew I had to leave this place, to return to my former life. It was one of the things I held onto in my thoughts, almost looked forward to the day that I would return to the United Kingdom.

I had decided to take up fiction writing, although I was afraid the only reason I was able to write so well was this place, and that it may be a gift I was unable to take back from the island.

I felt strong as I breathed in the fresh, light air around me. It made me feel more alive, as if I was healthier than I'd ever been in my life. Not one to spend time in gyms, I suppose I had not been in great shape when I left London in search of something more thrilling, something more beautiful than my constant surroundings of the hectic lifestyle. But now, after all the trekking and travelling and working – and yes, sometimes starving – I had put my body through, the weight had seemed to drop off me and I don't think I'd ever been so skinny in my adult life. The jeans that I'd worn for so long now hung off my body, my belt tied tight around my waist in order to keep them up.

Standing tall now in the darkness, the giant rubbery leaves cool on my skin, I also felt darkness within myself; as if Mandi's words had manifested it – or perhaps it had been there all along. However it was not a darkness that consumed me, more one that let me know exactly what I wanted. I was in control more than I'd ever been.

It was then I started to hear voices in the distance. I listened closely, frozen to the spot, unable to measure how far they were from me. I lost count of how many I heard but they were definitely male. One of them was shouting now, sounding agitated and angry yet the sound of the tide was making it difficult to hear their words.

I discretely checked the time on my digital camera – 01:02 am. The time did occur to me as odd, but I moved forward towards the edge of the trees as silently as possible to get a better look.

They had only just started to come ashore; I saw two boats, and some men starting to disembark. A chill went through my spine as I noticed their machine guns and the way they were dressed all in black. There was four of them, starting to lead others off the boat; they looked as if they were tied up, hands behind their backs and I could barely make out the tape over their mouths, but I knew it was there. A hostage situation? Why the hell are they bringing them here?

But I already knew the answer; isolation equals a good place to dump the bodies. No, I reasoned with myself, maybe just so they can't be found by the authorities. Yet somehow even then I knew the signs did not look good for these men.

All six hostages were now kneeling face-down on the beach, hands still tied behind their backs as one of the men with guns started to shout at them in Thai. I watched as he poked his gun into one of their backs, as if to provoke an answer.

As if in answer to my thoughts I saw one of the gunmen remove the tape from the captives' mouths, yet still none of them dared to make a sound.

I had a very bad feeling as I watched the next few minutes unfold, yet I stood glued to the spot, unable to find a way to help. I hadn't even brought my mobile phone – it remained at the hostel back on the mainland.

I noticed one of the men seemed to be in charge – the leader, if you will – he was standing apart from the rest with what seemed like a remote radio. Even in the darkness I could tell that he was very muscular and towered over the other men.

One of the other men called him over, and I heard the name 'Amon'. That was his name, and it suited him, I thought to myself as I watched him walk over to the other male, who seemed to be in a heightened state of agitation. At one point he seemed almost to be pleading with Amon about something, but Amon shouted at him in a disgusted voice. At that point I wished I'd learnt more than a few phrases in Thai.

So far, none of them seemed to think the island was any less than deserted, which meant that for now I was safe. But all thoughts of myself quickly swept away as I noticed one of the hostages was trying to get up, the look on his face the picture of terror. He looked quite young, and a sense of dread and foreboding filled my stomach as I watched two of the 'guards' walk over to him and kick him down.

One of them shouted something in Thai and the second guard seemed to be arguing with them. With the distraction of the guard, the young looking hostage started to get up. I watched as he stumbled towards the opening in the forest – towards me.

The guards noticed his getaway and Amon shouted at the arguing guard, who quickly shut up. The hostage was still stumbling towards my hiding place as one of the guards began to follow Amon's instruction and just before the shot went off, I could swear the young captive looked right at me, seemingly in shock at what he saw. The fear on his face sank into my heart.

And then the shots went off, making me feel as if I wanted to throw up. I looked away as the boy was shot down screaming – killed right in front of my eyes. One of the other hostages – a man, perhaps the boy's father – got up, screaming as if in protest he stumbled towards the boy and was also shot down, collapsing near the first body. His blood started to seep in the sands and I kneeled there frozen, still hidden from view but unable to move a single inch for the fear that had seized my heart.

Yet as two of Amon's men approached, I realised I had to move back, aware of the small chance that they would notice my presence in the trees. Terrified, I slowly inched my way back into the vegetation, careful not to disturb too much of the thick mud under my feet. I held my breath as, still visible they pulled the bodies back towards the others leaving a trail of blood, and dumped him down before the other hostages. It seemed an example had been made.

My heart beat thick and heavy in my chest, and I struggled to stay conscious as by now I was feeling severely light-headed. I struggled with myself to stay calm, yet thoughts were racing through my mind, unable to do a thing to alert the authorities.

All of a sudden a strong hand was forced over my mouth, pulling me backwards into the forest and I jolted, kicking to get away, wanting to scream. I was terrified as I realised one of the guards must have noticed my position and slipped behind me.

I was spun around violently, prepared to fight for my life when my eyes met with something entirely unexpected; the sight of Mandi looking the worst I'd ever seen him, sweat running down his forehead and eyes wide with fright. He still had his hand over my mouth, but slowly he pulled it away as I struggled to silently get my breath back.

"Are you okay?" He whispered, his arms on mine as he tried to calm me and I noticed most inappropriately that his hair was standing up in an almost comic look.

"I'm fine…they just killed someone. I saw it happen right in front of me and there was nothing I could do!" I whispered back, so grateful to see Mandi once again.

"Shhh!" He mouthed, as we listened intensely for what seemed like an age. We could still hear their voices, but after a while when we could be sure that they had not heard us, he spoke again.

"We have to get off this island, Night," he told me, as I gave him a confused look.

"How did you get here, how did you know?" I asked him. He sighed, and looked into my eyes with his dark ones.

"There had been rumours that day, and when I saw them leave I knew I had to follow because I could not let anything happen to you…it would have been my fault, you know," he told me, voice full of remorse for taking me to the island.

It was then I started to cry, silent tears falling down my face and he looked at me, trembling and gently wiped the falling tears from my cheeks. Then he took my hand and pulled me to my feet, and together - as silently as possible – we began to make our way across the small island forest, towards the other side of the beach.

Shaking as I walked, and steadied by Mandi, I have no idea how long it took us to cross the island. It felt like a long time, as carefully I put one foot in front of the other. It was of course dark and we didn't have the option of a light, so a few times our feet slipped or got caught.

When we'd almost reached the other side, Mandi motioned for me to stop and stay put. He wouldn't let me go any further, as he walked ahead towards the opening in the trees, checking that it was safe.

When it seemed to be, he walked out onto the sand cautiously looking around when suddenly he stopped. I thought at first that he was just trying to locate his brother's boat, but then slowly he raised his arms and I realised with a slow dread that he had been caught.

Frozen on the spot I crouched down low and listened as I heard them running towards us. I could hear them getting closer, part of myself arguing that I should stand and stop whatever was about to happen, the other part shaking in fear. Mandi tried to speak, but before he could get the first word out a loud shot filled the island and I watched with horror as Mandi started to fall to the ground.

One of the gunmen approached him and knelt down, checking his clothes and pockets before sounding unimpressed. During that time I knew that if he looked up even once, I was probably dead. He walked off, leaving us on our own – or so it seemed.

Shaking uncontrollably and struggling to keep down my hysteria, I slowly crawled over to where Mandi lay unconscious. He'd been shot in the chest, and I gently moved the hair away from his face, unsure of what to do next.

"Oh God..." I whispered as I cradled him in my arms, his blood already staining my clothes as I wildly looked around for the boat or anything that could save Mandi. I knew I wouldn't be able to live with myself if I let him die like this, for me.

I'd thought this side of the beach was deserted, but then I heard footsteps to my left and sharply I turned to see one of the men with guns approaching me. He looked deadly serious, his muscular arms shining in the moonlight.

He had large, serious eyes, a long straight nose and thick full lips. Terror seized me, froze me to the spot as I took in the information in front of me, and then he reached out to me, making me jump back from him.

"Hey...lady you have to get out of here!" He whispered with a strong urgency, and all I could do was stare at him in shock. I couldn't reply, or even move as I gripped Mandi's body even tighter.

"You have to at least hide, before they see you!" He told me again, before picking me up and physically dropping me back in the wilderness. He stared deep into my eyes to see if I comprehended what he was saying, and I realised that this was the man from earlier, the one who'd been arguing with Amon over presumably, the lives of the hostages.

"Who are you?" I whispered.

"I am Petri, you must stay here. The police are on their way, okay?" He told me with a cool, calm confidence.

"My friend…" I started to whisper, but he put his hand to my mouth as if to tell me not to make a sound, and then quickly stepped out of the bushes towards one of the approaching guards.

"Nothing here," he spoke to them in English. The guard muttered something in Thai and they started to walk back towards the other side of the beach.

I stayed there for a while, curled up in a ball as I fought to get control of my trembling body once more. I cried for Mandi and for the boy I'd seen killed before my eyes. I wasn't just scared, I was terrified and the island I'd so loved had become my worst nightmare.

What brought me back to reality were the shots, firing again and again from the far side of the beach. They made me feel sick, and after what seemed like forever there was silence; I knew then that none of the captives remained alive.

In the distance I registered the sound of a helicopter overhead, but nothing could penetrate my shock as I staggered to my feet. I walked cautiously in the darkness, through the island I'd got to know so well over the past couple of days.

I could hear voices yet they didn't sound right; somehow different, as if they chanted something mysterious and unknown. The further I walked, the closer they sounded and more confused my mind became. The chanting sounded urgent, loud and very spooky to my ears. Absent-mindedly I wiped my hand over my top, staining it with yet more of Mandi's blood. I felt weak, as if I might topple over yet somehow I kept walking, getting closer and closer to the voices in front of me.

When I finally reached the clearing, I silently recoiled at the sight of the bodies that littered the beach. In between the hostages I noticed that two of the gunmen had also been shot down, leaving a scene of gore I did not want to linger on for too long for the sake of my stomach.

Amon and another were sitting across a fire, and I realised that it was Amon chanting. The fire was burning brightly around them, and Amon held a small wooden object over it, chanting something repeatedly in desperate tones.

There was also a strange smell in the air, it was almost refreshing and seemed to awaken me enough that I didn't collapse there and then. I was in a deep shock, unable to register exactly what was going on around that fire.

The other man just seemed to sit – no slump there, as if he'd been put to sleep. After a few seconds I realised that it was Petri, his eyes shut he seemed to be hanging almost unnaturally over the fire as if at any given moment he would fall into it.

Amon's chanting was getting louder and more desperate, sending a deep chill down my spine. The increasingly loud whirr of the helicopter did not seem to penetrate his deep concentration as he shouted over the top of it.

I could see the helicopter approaching yet I could not take my eyes off Amon and Petri, who seemed to be transfixed by an almost paranormal activity. Their guns were laid down next to them upon the sand and they were both surrounded by the blood of the hostages and their own men. Amon appeared to have smeared some of the blood on his forehead, as it was now bright red.

His eyes were shut also and he had no idea that anyone was watching them, sweat pouring down his face, his shirt drenched. I could feel a large amount of heat radiating from the fire, as I stared transfixed.

Even as the helicopter touched down on the beach, Amon continued to chant, seemingly reaching a climax of sorts. The Thai police started to shout at them at first from the helicopter and then from a few feet away on the beach and suddenly whatever force Amon had been controlling was broken, his body seeming to slump to the ground.

Petri quickly looked alert and stood to his feet, following the instructions of the police he put his hands above his head as they rushed over to them. Amon, on the other hand was going wild in panic as he jumped back and staggered towards his gun.

His eyes looked wild and confused as he ran and tripped over the bodies, the sweat thick on his skin. He looked scared and groggy, almost clumsy as if he wasn't used to his own body. He was almost at his dead friend's machine gun, which made me question from somewhere far away in my mind, why he hadn't just gone for his own.

As the Thai police raised their guns to shoot, he turned and started to utter one word.

"N-no!" He shouted at the top of his lungs, but it was already too late.

Judging the situation somewhat promptly, the police shot him down as he screamed hysterically and I was unable to look away as he collapsed in a pool of his own blood, his hand landing only inches away from one of the gunmen that lay dead beside him.

After a few seconds of shock, I carefully stepped out of the trees in full view of the police, hands in the air and shaking uncontrollably.

Petri turned to look at me and his expression shocked me; an almost cold smile as his stony eyes took me in, before the authorities had pinned him down and cuffed him on the sand. I couldn't stay in the situation for any longer as my body finally gave in and I passed out to the view of dark figures running towards me.

That scene has stuck in my mind as I run through it over and over again. I should have read the signs, yet even the possibility of what had become reality was far too insane for me to even begin to take in.

But when he smiled at me, on the beach, surrounded by the blood and the bodies – something definitely seemed wrong. When I first awoke I thought I'd imagined what I'd seen, but in these eternal moments since my passing that one second played over in my memory and I became convinced that that smile had been real.

But I suppose that in my post-horror traumatic life, my second chance had been filled with selfishness, an overwhelming hunger to return back home – to London, where I could let things return to normal or at least what passes for normal back there.

I wanted to forget more than anything the scenes that I'd witnessed, the horror of death that had touched my heart like a cold icicle. I tried to fill my life with warmth, yet I could not forget and in my fiction – oh yes, I continued my fiction for a time – it showed.

In the short months before my death I can even say that I became something of a success in the writing world, with everyone curious to hear of the moments where my life supposedly flashed before my eyes.

'Terror Thailand' had made the national newspapers, and my extended article on Thailand even won an award. Somehow these small tokens of acceptance, things I'd wanted quite a lot before my travels, didn't seem to cheer me much and I spent more time holed up in my small apartment, chained to my computer.

I continued to write my fiction, which had become dark and twisted, until the moment when my life was taken away from me. Ignoring my publishing deal, a book about my travels, I instead spent my precious time writing about a serial killer's thoughts as he killed again and again.

I didn't feel like myself, stuck in my own little bubble, a false comfort against the outside world. I didn't think that this bubble I'd created was doing more harm to me, to my mind, than I'd ever thought possible. It made me forget. I never bothered to wonder about my writing, where the thoughts came from that were all of a sudden spilling out like a waterfall onto the paper. I told myself that the trauma of the past events had changed me somehow as if my old self would never – could never – return. Yet in passing, from time to time Mandi's words about the dark still echoed softly in my mind.

I stayed up late at nights, typing away on my computer until that fated night when all would become dark forever…

Chapter Nine

When clarity once again entered my mind I became clear that I must leave Magnus's room. It was a place I would no doubt return to, but right then it was also a place I had to leave be. So I left.

I left behind his books, possessions and old dusty boxes that he'd once treasured more in death than in life, and I looked ahead to the thin-paned window that beckoned me into the night sky.

I don't know what I was looking for when I immersed myself into the unknown, away from my terrible isolation and into the harsh winds of London. I still don't know, but in my mind I knew it was what I needed.

At first my spirit felt weak, as if it would break in the wind and scatter into a million pieces so that I could never feel any pain or emotion ever again; so that I'd never be me.

Once I'd got over the wind and began to feel my strength return, I looked down upon the beautiful lights and landmarks of London, my old home. If I had any breath in me, it would have been taken away by that sight, and as I stayed in that spot, completely transfixed, I whispered to my teacher.

"Look Magnus, life goes on," I didn't wait for a response before I rushed through the air, taking in the sights and sounds closer to the ground. I soon found my old confidence that I'd gained with my teacher, sapping strength from my living hosts and enjoying the vibrant nightlife that the city had to offer me.

To feel that way again was as if my soul had been mended; cleansed in a way that I did not know was possible. It occurred to me that maybe I had never been broken at all.

I was drawn to a band playing that night, the heavy metal filling the air like electricity in the venue as the crowd jumped and rocked out almost like a collective. I felt I could be one with the music, it's beauty overtaking me with my new senses running amok. I could almost see the vibrations in the air. I stayed there until the very end of the gig, temporarily forgetting my limitations I felt part of the crowd, almost like I belonged once more.

I saw no spirits that night, but I know now that they noticed me as I let my energy take over and almost danced in the wind. So many people moving all around me, every single mind individual and special yet so ordinary at the same time. I was mesmerised by life although I knew it was something that I'd never be part of again.

Sadness entered my heart for barely seconds before it was flushed away by happiness at the world around me and I left London to explore and lose myself in my surroundings.

I must have 'flown' for hours, unable to stop myself from spending my apparently boundless energy and taking in everything around me as if I could absorb each sight like a sponge.

The wind grew harsher around me the further north I found myself, until at last I stopped in utter shock as I felt him around me once more. Magnus, his touch…I closed my eyes and felt him there for what seemed like a small eternity but then suddenly he was gone and in front of me a light glowed off in the distance. I reasoned with myself afterwards that it had been nothing but the wind.

Shortly afterwards another light appeared beside the first, then another and another yet they were surrounded by mist, glowing dimly ahead of me. There was no way to tell how far they lay but it struck me as odd that they should suddenly appear so high in the sky.

The lights I thought to myself, yet shrugged this feeling away as I tried to reach them with all my remaining strength. As time went on, I thought that this couldn't possibly be true, how far away could these lights lie? It felt like I would never reach them, forever the same distance apart from my soul.

Tormenting, cruel lights…surely they were waiting for me? I felt myself growing weaker as faster I tried to travel towards the beacons shining more brightly in front of me now. But I had lost my bearings and knew nothing of distance anymore; all I cared of was the lights.

Yet soon it became clear to me that it was close to sunrise and all my strength and substance would be stripped from me until nightfall. I felt the sun start its ascent and at the same time felt myself grow weaker and starting to fade.

I felt frustration as the lights were gradually, cruelly being taken away from me like everything else had been. Eventually I gave up, unable to carry on as I faded into the light, losing my sight of the fading glow ahead of me.

When I woke once more I found myself back in Magnus's room; an inexplicable truth yet it was somewhere I had formed a deep emotional attachment to. So, in a way I was stuck here.

Anger flooded my mind and I rushed out through the window once more into the cold air of the night, searching desperately for the sight of the lights. It was London, a city full of lights yet none of these were my lights.

In an increasing state of agitation I rushed north once more frantically hoping to catch sight of them, that they'd take me away to where I was really supposed to be. It occurred to me that maybe they already knew that I wasn't ready to give it up yet. Angrily I brushed this thought away and found myself instead racing towards the old church that Magnus had taught me in.

As I approached the old stained glass windows I half expected to see the same old woman waiting in the pews, but alas the church was silent and empty. I'm not sure if I was completely relieved at this sight, as even an old screaming witch seemed better than my own company at that time.

All the candles were unlit, set out on the table in the same way that Magnus had left them for our lesson. I felt an overwhelming sense of grief as I remembered the things he had taught me that night, and all my anger and frustrations built up inside of me until I screamed as loud as I possibly could.

When finally I had let out my energy and my soul felt weak I looked around the church again as if seeing it for the first time, and noticed straight away that the candles had been lit.

The information went through me like a lightning bolt and I turned around sharply to see two figures standing before me. The first figure was of a man wearing a black trench coat and a brightly coloured scarf. His hair was short and black and his eyes a deep dark brown colour, his skin a pale olive. Dark stubble stood out on his chin, as if he had not shaved before his death. Beside him, holding his hand was a young blonde girl who looked no more than seven years of age, her pale blue eyes glinting in the dimly lit room. At once I could tell they were dead, like me and that they could also see me.

It was a deep shock, the first souls I'd seen in weeks since Magnus had so abruptly left me. I staggered on what to say to either of them, before the man spoke up.

"Forgive me, but Claudia does not like the dark," he gestured towards the candles, a serious but polite expression on his face.

"That's-that's okay," I stuttered as I looked at the vacant expression on the girl's pallid face.

"We don't mean to intrude, but we have been watching you," his accent was European and thick, "We dwell in this area too and your behaviour has been…unsettling to my little girl. She thinks that you look like her mummy, because of course it's been so long since she has last seen her mother."

"Oh…I'm sorry," I didn't really know what else to say. The man's expression seemed to grow more heated and I recoiled. He let go of the girl and swept towards me as if his feet did not even move from the floor. He pointed his finger at me, his scarf blowing back from his neck as he seemed to be generating a breeze all around him. It started to feel warmer in the room.

"You!" He shouted, "You look just like her!" He stared at me dangerously with his angry eyes, before a look of sorrow overcame him and a tear dripped down his cheek. The little girl stood in the same position, now clutching a white teddy bear to her chest and looking fear-stricken. He shouted at me again.

"She walked into the light just like you were trying to do; only she made it! SHE MADE IT! Why couldn't it have been you instead of her?!" He looked enraged at me and for one moment I thought that he could actually harm me, before he retreated back to looking plain sad.

He started to walk back, muttering and grabbing the girl's hand as she looked back at me, her long blonde hair blowing in the breeze.

"You look just like her...Beatrice," he muttered just before I saw them disappear through the old brick wall of the church and into the churchyard. I occurred to me they'd probably forgotten exactly what this Beatrice looked like.

As soon as they'd left, the candles blew out leaving me in the darkness once more. I knew that I had not imagined their presence, as I stood there chilled to the bone but what had I done that was so intrusive? The man's haunted eyes remained etched into my memory, making me feel threatened and ill at ease. I called to Magnus for help, but of course no help came.

"You left me here! I can't deal with any of this without you, Magnus!" I shouted to the empty church, to the darkness in between each pew. There was nothing around me but silence and cool musty air.

And just like the man who'd lost his wife, I sounded angry as hell. But I soon realised there was absolutely nothing I could do to bring Magnus back, yet I felt as if there was a massive part of myself missing – like a hole in the heart. I felt weak.

My self destructiveness kicked in once more and I felt the emotions taking over me, the familiar heat building up inside and I let it take over me – yes, I made the conscious decision to let it – and with that I fed it and felt it take over me, pushing out as the fire took over the small church, consuming it in flames.

I could see the thick grey smoke all around me and I stood there, arms out to embrace it although of course, it could not touch me. The bright orange flames grew and I tried to imagine what it had felt like, for Viola to die in those flames; the agony, the struggle to breathe in fresh, clean air, the suffocation. I wondered for how long she had been conscious, if she had now passed to the light. I wished I could die like that; I deserved to die the way I'd killed Viola, alas my time to die had already passed. Perhaps I would be punished here in the dark to replay the memories over, and over…I was smiling now, almost laughing at my situation. At least Viola got her husband back, or so I could imagine as the church began to disintegrate around me.

Perhaps she and Magnus were together now, like the old times where they had once loved each other – and he had loved her with all of his heart. I'd read his journals, jealously and anger difficult to control although I could bear it for the knowledge that then he was mine.

Now all I had to look forward to was nothingness. It made my soul ache, the old pity for myself sinking in once more as I thought back to the night with the candles, and Magnus's expression on his face. He'd told me to stay away from the others, and now I had only angered them.

I stood there shaking, unsure of what to do as I hadn't been aware I'd disrupted any of the spirits – never even seen any other spirits for so long until tonight when they came to me. I stayed in the old church for a short time, watching it slowly collapse before heading back into the night. I suppose it had been a holy place in terms of my memories in this side of the dark, and I felt a pang of sorrow as I saw it burn surrounded by darkness, smoke clouding the sky. I looked around briefly for the two spirits from the church. I saw nothing, although I began to think I'd probably angered them more. At least the girl could look at the pretty flames that lit up the darkness like a friendly torch. I doubted her father would agree with my idea, and I wondered if they would return to chase me away.

As the church faded away in the distance I felt like my world was becoming smaller and smaller, as if I'd be stuck in the small room until the end of time. I wished for the courage to find something more.

It began to occur to me that perhaps I did not possess whatever it was that allowed me to find other souls, or to find the lights; perhaps last night had been a fluke.

I began to wonder that perhaps I was stuck in this state forever, and that any spirit that crossed my path would be ready and eager to fight me. I welcomed insanity but before it would arrive I knew that I had to find more spirits like the ones I'd seen tonight. The thought of other spirits brightened my mood; perhaps they would be more helpful and allow me to find a way to come to terms with Magnus, and to find the elusive bright lights.

Chapter Ten

I had been back in Satun for two days, then four days, then two weeks and I still felt numb from the shock of what had happened. Most of the time had been spent with the authorities as I gave my witness statement and relived those moments over and over in my mind. I was referred to a British psychologist who had dealt with similar cases in the past, his name was Tony Bennett.

Although he had incredible tact he was also used to questioning backpackers and holidaymakers who had been through similar trauma and some of his questions just didn't seem the kind I expected to answer. He took me by surprise, with his shock of blonde hair and bright blue eyes and for short intervals at a time all that seemed to exist was me and him in a small room. And for a time, that was just fine with me. I found it hard to think of the outside world.

The story had made the news back home in Britain, and I received calls from worried family and friends, who made plans to bring me back from Thailand ASAP. To me it was all a blur, although I'd eventually got a call from my mother who could not bear for me to be alone there any longer, she was catching a flight the next day. She was a strong woman who despised being told to wait for anything longer than two minutes.

Now I think of it, I wonder how she coped with my death; knowing her she was probably campaigning for mother's rights or for my killer to be sent down forever. Or both, but never mind that for now. This story lies back in Satun.

Luckily Mandi had managed to hold onto his struggle for life and had now been released from hospital early, mostly due to his unbreakable spirit and pure willpower. Most of his strength was now recovered although he still bore the scars and dressing from a punctured lung, broken rib and internal bleeding. I was grateful that he was still alive, although apart from my one visit in hospital I felt it difficult to talk to him about what had happened.

That's why it was hard to approach Mandi on the beach that day as I stood there watching him staring out to the sea, large sunglasses covering his eyes.

I knew there was something of incredible importance I had to do before I left Thailand for good, or I would never be rested. My thinking on this particular subject started literally just hours after being rescued from the island, sitting in a small dirty room, waiting to be questioned. Even though I couldn't stop shaking from the trauma and the shock of seeing the murders, I felt regret at leaving behind my leather-bound book.

Of course I was grateful to have my life and felt an overwhelming relief when I discovered Mandi was still alive, but this book was not just the ordinary travel diaries I had been accustomed to writing. It was fiction, actual fiction – I'd never been able to write anything barely readable that was not my own experience but on the island my imagination just seemed to flow and I grew addicted to the story.

All the same, to be able to retrieve the book I needed help, and getting there without question would prove very difficult. It was almost crazy for me to want to return to the island where I'd witnessed such horror, but at the same time it felt like I'd left part of myself behind.

I walked down the beach towards Mandi, the wind blowing back my hair and my white caftan revealing my bikini underneath. I bore no real scars from the island; my skin was still as pure and unblemished as it always had been. Still, I didn't really feel like myself, as if I wasn't really in my own body.

As I got closer, he turned to look at me and although I could not read his eyes, a small smile formed on his lips. He looked relaxed as ever, only the bandages over his chest revealed what he had recently been through. It hurt my heart to see them and realise it was my fault for leading him there.

"Hi," I said, unsure exactly what to say next, "How are you holding up?"

He laughed, "They put me back together again, Night. I'm just like humpty-dumpty."

I laughed too, more because his accent didn't really go with 'humpty-dumpty' more than anything else; it just sounded wrong.

"I'm so sorry Mandi," I began, as he slowly took his glasses off, "I wish I'd never mentioned…you know; it's my fault you went there."

I could see his deep brown eyes now and he looked at me sadly. I realised there was not much more I could say, and nothing I could say to make it better. A small tear began to run down my cheek.

"Hey, hey! None of that please! Now, let's go and get a milkshake, alright?"

So we walked together and sat at the small café where we'd first met, looking out at the beautiful beach and the people that crowded it like only tourists can.

We talked for what seemed like hours, the subject of the book always in the back of my mind. It became more pressing to me how close I was to going back home. Eventually Mandi began to notice and as if giving me a helping hand he addressed my silence.

"Night," Mandi spoke, bringing me out of my thoughts, "What is on your mind? There is something you want to say, no?"

I sighed heavily, trying to find the words to explain how I was feeling, but no words came.

"I left something behind that night…something very important to me," I spoke softly, before looking up to judge his reaction. He looked confused.

"What did you leave?" he asked me, looking uncomfortable in his chair. Okay, now it was time.

"I left my book…you won't understand," I said, shaking my head, "it had so many things that were important to me, things that came straight from my soul. I put a lot of work into that book."

He nodded, silently as if to consider my words. As to what would come next, he knew it I'm sure.

"Look," I told him, unable to look into his eyes, "you don't have to come, but if you could only lend me the boat one last time I'll go back there myself."

He turned to me sharply; his eyes looked angry yet inside him was his usual deep calm.

"I cannot let you do that, Night," he spoke, coolly but firmly. I opened my mouth to speak, to try and find a way to persuade him of my urgency knowing that it had been a stupid thing to ask for, but then I realised he had not finished.

"I'll go with you."

I sat back in my chair in shock, and looked deep into his eyes to make sure he meant it, unable to understand why he would do such a thing for me. As if he knew what I was thinking, he answered my internal question.

"I can't let you go alone, but I promise you I will not set foot on that island." I understood. And so it was agreed that we would leave for the island. It had to be done quickly so I left the café that day with Mandi to fetch his brother's boat; the boat that had not been used since its last trip to the small island – my island of deadly paradise.

During the time that we walked and started to set up the boat, it didn't really seem real. I hadn't expected Mandi to allow this so easily or even at all and I had never in my wildest dreams thought in reality that I'd return to the island one last time.

Mandi was silent for most of the preparation and as we readied to leave, some of the locals gave us glances; none of them challenged us.

It was around noon when we left the beach towards the islands, the situation still surreal to me as I watched the beautiful clear water ripple around us in mild waves. I looked back at the beautiful sands of the beach and gave a wary smile.

It felt as if we were in a dream that day, as Mandi guided us through the seemingly endless waters towards the islands.

Why he brought me there that day, I do not know. He appeared wary of the island now, as he looked across the sea with a kind of faraway gaze.

It seemed like we'd travelled far when we finally reached the island's sands, and as the boat touched upon the shore, Mandi was true to his word; he would not leave the boat.

"I want you to find that book, and come straight back here, okay? Listen to me, do not look around or linger more than you have to. There are ghosts on this island."

I turned to him, shocked by his words but his expression told me to hurry. At first I walked quickly, and then started to run across the beach.

Even though there had been an investigation, the Thai authorities had soon left the beach as it had been, looking untouched by blood and crime; that's the way they like to preserve the islands, which I supported greatly.

Soon I found my marker tree, looking like an old friend I'd abandoned long ago. It stood there lonely as I approached it now at walking speed. Would my book still be there? None of the authorities had questioned me about a book, and surely if they'd found it they would have returned it to me or kept it for evidence.

Since Amon and most of the other gang members had been killed, only Petri was left a subject of their interrogation. I was able to testify that Petri had tried to help me escape the island, and Thai police found that he had been forced onto the island that night.

He remained silent mostly, in shock and severely traumatised by the events that we'd both witnessed. I never directly spoke to Petri, or found out what happened to him after I left the island.

The only thing I remembered about him was his serious, caring eyes and the way he looked that night when he told me to stay in hiding. He very possibly saved my life.

I knelt down beside the tree, looking carefully in the sand for the place I had left the white rock. Carefully moving the sand away with my fingers I found the rock easily. Underneath lay the book that I had left there on the last night; so the authorities had not swept the island clean completely.

Running my fingers over the leather of the book made me feel odd, sending an involuntary shiver down my spine. I opened it to see the handwriting of my old self, looking somehow naïve as I described my travels in Bangkok and before that, Malaysia. I had never liked looking back on my handwriting, it always looked somehow wrong to me.

I could still hear the waves crashing upon the shore as I knelt down on the soft white sands, almost hearing what could be whispers within the sounds of the beach.

I closed the book, and standing up I was almost ready to go back to the boat, but ahead of me just a little further to the right the sand looked odd, disturbed. As I got closer I realised it was where Amon had started the fire on that night, and I remembered the strange chanting. The words chilled me all over again, but I still had no idea what he had been saying. I remembered Petri, who had seemed dazed and sleepy as he sat across from Amon at the fire; something registered within me that told me it was not right.

I ran my fingers along the sand, finding traces of burnt wood and ash that had not yet been buried under the sand by the wind. I frowned as my fingers seemed to catch on something else, and as I picked it out of the sand I felt a deep chill settle in my bones.

It was a sort of charm, a black charred wooden doll on a black thick piece of leather, tied in a knot at the back. The doll looked unexplainably evil as it stared back at me, and I dusted off the remaining grains of sand.

Had it been the same charm that Amon had been holding on that particular night, above the fire? I thought so, and that gave me a cold feeling in my heart as I looked at it in the hot sun. Even though it felt wrong to take it, I did not want to leave the charm there alone on the island, could not or would not put it back in the sand.

Remembering what Mandi had told me I quickly (almost guiltily) pocketed the figure and looked up to the boat across the other end of the beach. I expected to see Mandi sitting there, but the boat was empty. Quickly standing up I looked around searching for Mandi's familiar figure; perhaps he had decided to take a walk along the beach after all? But something about that thought seemed to ring false.

Stumbling across the sands I almost broke into a run towards the boat, glancing around at the wildlife and hoping not to have to enter the wilderness once again to look for him.

The next time I looked at the boat I got a shock; Mandi was right there, waiting for me just as I had left him, visible on the end of the boat.

He registered the fear in my eyes and looked guarded as he asked me what happened.

"Are you alright?" he asked, concern showing in his expression.

"I'm fine," I said, jumping back into the small boat with my book under one arm, "Let's go."

I never looked back as we left the island for the last time. A couple of times I kept in touch with Mandi via email and as far as I know, his fear allowed so that he never used the boat again.

Chapter Eleven

I started my search to find new souls with an almost innocent eloquence and naivety that even now I remember with a painful clarity. I was once again confused by the world of the dead, and my place in it. Where were these strange creatures, how did they exist? It annoys me to think of the time when I thought I was being cautious, a creature of the dark. Really, truthfully, I craved the attention and prayed for answers to my selfish questions without a second thought to disturbing their world.

For surely there must be others out there like me, who seek answers or perhaps have already found them? To me it was like I was looking into their world from the outside, a lavish party that I had not been invited to. Could it be that there were others out there, alone in the dark? I thought so, and with that attitude I set out into the skies, searching for any glimmer of a soul. I had senses, although the little teaching I'd received only uncovered the very tip of what I could feel deep down; I was like a volcano waiting to erupt, my disgrace still fresh in my thoughts. Magnus.

Little did I know that at the same time of my search, I was exposing my vulnerability, opening myself up to them in invitation. I may have been stronger than when I first discovered this new world, but I was still weak and still utterly clueless in terms of its rules.

The wind rushed through me once more as I struggled to feel complete within myself, the familiar feeling of being pushed ten different ways enveloping me entirely.

But then I felt something new, different; I stiffened as a conscious coldness passed through me and the words, barely there whispered through the night air. However I was not scared; it gave me hope as I listened to its message.

'The Cobra' it whispered, 'Feel it. Come now' I turned sharply to the sound of the voices as they whispered around me, but once again I felt nothing more than wind. Who had been there, had whispered so harshly in my ear? I found myself alone, looking over towards the Cobra Hotel.

The hotel itself was old and almost shabby in its appearance, but yes, I could feel it. Inside, someone was waiting with one particular spot standing out to me. How I knew this came as a mystery to me and I realised that this was yet another thing I had to learn.

Under my breath I cursed Magnus for leaving me an incomplete, barely there moron who second-guessed how to use her own spiritual body. But of course, I had let myself be seen and that accounted for something. I felt useless, and suddenly also very afraid at making the next move.

The room within the hotel waited for me ominously, and taking a chance I made the decision to pay whoever was there a visit. After all, it would have been rude not to.

On the way there I let my thoughts flood around me, unsure of how to proceed or what to expect from this…entity whose presence felt stronger the closer I allowed myself to get.

I entered the room in full force, welcomed by elegant surroundings and a warm atmosphere. The carpet was a thick cream pile and extravagant light fixtures lit up the room perfectly; not somewhere I'd expect to be haunted.

A beautiful bed draped in satin and velvet was the focal point of the room, taking up the centre space as if it belonged there. The room appeared empty, and as I looked around at the elaborate tapestries that hung from the walls, the mahogany chest where candles rested and sleeping cats lay as if miniatures of life, I felt a change in the room.

Turning swiftly I gazed upon the figure elegantly rested on the king-sized bed; had she been there all along? I thought so, yet how she had hidden I do not know.

She wore a black lace-stitched evening dress that hung over the satin like dark water coming alive all around her. A black velvet choker hung across her neck, dark red lips almost the colour of blood making her pale face come alive...and of course the eyes, a deep purple had me frozen to the spot.

"I know what you're thinking," she spoke, a deep voice cut like velvet through the air and I detected a hint of bitterness, "My name is Gabrielle. You came here for answers, even if you would not admit it to yourself. I know you, Night. You want to know truth, do you not?"

I nodded, confused but before I could speak I felt a breeze as the two spirits that'd apprehended me earlier entered the room. They looked different to the way I expected, their skin tones a deep olive and their hair jet black and cut short. I only caught a slight glimpse of hazel brown eyes as they passed me.

"Yusif, Tariq, leave us alone now, she is safe," they acknowledged Gabrielle and avoided my stare as they moved through the building. Yusif had a goatee and wore a military jacket, while Tariq looked much younger and wore a hooded top. Of course, age matters not in this version of life as we know it...or in some cases maybe not.

Still, it didn't seem to fit Gabrielle's image, and I pondered on what exactly was going on before my silence was filled with Gabrielle's thickly feminine voice once more.

"Night, we have rules. You must follow these rules as does every member of the non-living, earth dwelling spirits," she looked at me sternly, her pale skin a contrast to her dark black hair cut drastically short. A longish trail of a curl had fallen onto her forehead and her hands rested at either side of her dress in an understated elegance that far surpassed anything I'd seen in modern London.

"Who are you, Gabrielle? I am sorry but my master failed to teach me these things," I spoke up with my own bitter tone, causing my host to look up incredulous. Then she smiled.

"Ah, yes, you knew Magnus," she told me, her voice rising slightly with his name, "We'll get back to him. Normally I would not do this as most spirits are harmless; lost and confused. You however, have been causing quite a stir."

I stood quietly indignant as if waiting for her point. This seemed to silently infuriate her, her lips drawing tighter together, her pale skin almost glowing in the well-lit room. I guessed she must have been around twenty-nine when she passed, although I was at a loss to which century that had been.

At last she continued with her speech.

"I understand you have the power of fire…quite unusual but then you learned from the best I suppose," she spoke coldly, softly, her eyes wandering around the room before resting suddenly on me again, "You cannot go around destroying things, killing mortals!"

Her voice has risen dramatically and suddenly I grew very uneasy of her company, her eyes burning into mine like purple liquid mercury.

"Magnus did not make me aware of these 'rules', I don't have to do anything that you ask of me because you owe me nothing!" I retaliated, much to her surprise and almost pleasure.

"Magnus was a good friend of mine, although of course he had the same, irresponsible and volatile attitude," she spoke softly, "Nevertheless, he was a very gentle and misunderstood soul and I understand your actions caused him to move on."

She stared at me until I showed some kind of response, and unable to look at her I moved towards the window. Outside drops of rain fell out of the night sky, the moon showing fully despite the clouds.

I spoke up, angrily, "What happened between Magnus and I was nothing to do with you, nothing! What the hell do you want from me, Gabrielle?" She laughed at me, at my anger.

"You are foolish, young one," she said, menacingly, "You have much to learn. But however foolish, you must not interfere with life or cause it to end for mortals."

I shook my head as her words raced around my mind, and yet something else occurred to me.

"You said you could read my thoughts, is this true?" I asked her.

"Yes, it's true," she replied, "But I am much stronger than you."

"Perhaps you can show me? I swear, I was unaware there were rules on how I exist, I feel stuck in between worlds as if my existence should end here. I am the first to admit, I need help."

She nodded as if to agree, as if she almost felt sorry for my display of desperation and loneliness.

"You are promising Night, perhaps I could teach you what I know and give you the answers you most desire, my love. But first you must say you understand what I have told you."

"But I don't…I mean I did not intend to use my talents in such a destructive way. I still need to come to terms with this existence."

"Of course. You were a journalist who found out a little too much, no?" She looked at me in a way I did not understand, and stupidly I asked her.

"What are you talking about?"

"Never mind," her manner seemed to change swiftly as she rose up from the bed, the long black lace of her dress almost hypnotising as it moved over the soft fabrics, "I can tell you nothing that will be of help to you concerning your former life. It's more important now to teach you of this side of the dark, the things you yearn to know all about."

Although she was slightly mocking in the way she spoke to me, almost cruelly, I ignored her comment. I was desperate to learn the things she knew, to be able to understand the reasons why I was there.

When she stood there before me it hit me that she was utterly beautiful, an exquisite creature that'd somehow been trapped in the same place as me in this peculiar situation. Yet something did not seem right, the way she almost commanded those two souls to her and how they seemed to obey every word she said.

Her black lace trailed across the floor as she grew closer to me, and again it seemed as if she was reading my thoughts.

"I am strong, it is a difficult ability to master," she said while nodded, seeming to understand exactly what I was thinking.

"Was Magnus able to read thoughts too?" I asked her, thinking of the times that he was kind yet guarded of his feelings.

"No, but he could read feelings, if he pushed himself," Gabrielle replied, before continuing, "There is of course, a way where you can close yourself off to other souls; so that they cannot feel you or read your thoughts. You know how to conceal yourself, don't you Night?"

I nodded, although I wasn't entirely sure how well I could carry off this particular ability; it had been second nature after Magnus warned me of the others.

"Did he warn you of me? No, I can tell he did not," Gabrielle seemed to consider her options, her cold hand touching my arm as if we were both physical beings.

"Yes, there are dangers out there my dear, so you must be more wary than you have been. Close your mind so it becomes hard and insignificant, cold like a stone," she told me, her accent very hard to read. She smiled, and somehow I gathered that she had been French once, long ago. This frightened me, the way the thought just seemed to become knowledge to my mind even though I had never heard her voice.

She took my hand and I felt a warmth surge through me, just as if I had been alive once more.

"How did…what just happened?" I asked her, confused.

"I will show you, child." She replied, a kindness in her voice that had not been there before.

I still do not know why she agreed to teach me these things; perhaps she saw something in me that she'd once seen in herself. After all, I showed 'promise'.

She kept hold of my hand and soon after I found myself on the roof of the hotel, the wind blowing around us as her black lace danced around her like liquid mercury. The great London skyline shimmered around us, the roads beneath us busy with people and sounds, the smoke of cars forever polluting the air all around.

As part of my tutoring she told me of her previous life; not all of it, god forbid, but just enough that she was able to trust me with. It had been full of glamour and excitement yet it was a time where she craved for more…

She had been a part of the theatre many years before, a Paris star that had shimmered in black; always in black. People travelled from all around to view her plays, her beautiful pale skin always standing out just like a true star in the night.

She always played a particular kind of character, incredibly desirable yet at the same time cold and intelligent with skin that looked as white as snow.

Gabrielle Sonata's voice filled the theatres with beauty and melodic charms that anyone would wish to pay for, a true treasure of the critics she rose in popularity among the masses.

Yet she had been brutally murdered in her dressing room on the final night of her grandest play. It had been in the least, unexpected, the murder weapon still hidden beneath the once-bloodstained floorboards of the Coupe D'or Theatre.

The killer had been a dangerous and murderous obsessive whose advances had been refused by Gabrielle. Of course she'd had no need for his affection; the great actress whose dressing room never failed to fill with flowers.

As she lay dying in a pool of her own blood her soul had filled with venom and hated, the killer ripping a gold locket from her neck as a small memento of his 'love'.

"I was pulled into the spirit world full of darkness and hate, my desire for his death growing with every minute. I watched his movements forever trying to hurt or scare him, yet it took tremendous effort back then for anything like that," Gabrielle told me as I listened, transfixed to her tragic story, the disgust for her frailty showing in her voice, "Eventually when my hate grew strong enough I was able to terrify the murdering bastard but then it was too late and I went way beyond what I thought I was capable of doing; I killed him, violently, but somehow that did not seem to satisfy my needs the way I thought it would. I wanted my locket, and I wanted to punish the world that just seemed to move on long after my death. There was no way for me to do this, of course but I was maddened by grief for what I once was, and angry at the world."

As she moved towards the edge of the building, she continued the story, her voice like velvet enchanting me and her touch still fresh in my mind; I felt goose bumps as I recalled it.

"Tilly Loveridge took what would have been my role at the theatre…she was never a match for me. Innocent, blonde and stupid the bitch could never have the mental capacity to appreciate such a play. Her voice was hollow and lacked emotion, anything she did was half-baked and there she was, playing my role in one of the most beautiful plays of our time! Well, she never got to appreciate it much," she laughed, a chilly, empty sound.

"You killed her too?" I asked, knowing the answer even though it had never passed her lips. She turned to me with a look of anger and revulsion, and I once again saw the fire in her eyes.

"After that I found a better cause, a new revelation and it changed my spirit entirely," Gabrielle continued, "Instead of wallowing in self pity, I began to focus more on the dead. To…take advantage of the position I now found myself in, as it were."

She ran a long, sharp fingernail over the skin on her chest, seemingly enthralled at the paleness of her own body. She reminded me of a cat, a well-groomed predator.

"You said you'd teach me," I told her, not curious enough to endure her next fixation. She motioned with her hand in a nonchalant manner.

"Yes, yes and you have a lot to learn. Let us begin," she replied, her voice changing to one of confidence and passion. It was as if she had found her subject and was about to pounce.

"Imagine the wind, the very air around you is full of tiny particles; you have to make yourself join these particles, separate yourself into not one thing but many and this will conceal you from the others. Yes, some of the stronger souls will sense you or just a strong feeling, I will be able to sense you but your thoughts will be unreadable and most spirits will not notice your passing.

I listened to her words, unbelieving that it was possible and at first I was scared to separate in her way, imagine if I was unable to return to my spiritual form? I would be useless.

"This method is best used for travelling at speeds and…well escaping from those you do not wish to associate with. Don't worry, it will become second nature," her attempt to reassure me failed somewhat, but I still I tried to regain the feeling I'd experience earlier when Gabrielle took my hand.

At first I felt nothing, as if I was a solid block unable to move with the wind the way Gabrielle had so well described. The way she had forcibly fused with my soul still had me confused, but soon I was able to move at short distances apart the way I had with Gabrielle controlling me.

"Very good," she praised me now, watching my every move with an impenetrable look on her icy, expressionless face. It felt odd being taught once more by another soul, someone who was obviously stronger and coldly intelligent; I think I admired her.

"Tell me how I read thoughts, please Gabrielle," I now asked of her with a desperation and thirst for knowledge that I had not known since the first week of university, my living days. She smiled as if predicting my request.

"All in good time, Night," she replied to me, a patience in her voice that seemed to denote that she was for now settled, "I am closed to you, my private thoughts available not to a soul. There are others whom I must introduce you to, come."

With that she jumped from the ledge but instead of falling or floating in the air, she disappeared entirely. I used the method she had taught me and detecting a sense of something almost unreadable I followed it until she appeared in front of me, her haunted smile once again visible to me. She was still in the same long black dress, her milk-white chest almost luminous showing from her low neckline.

"Look at that man, that sad little soul, pathetic is he not?" She pointed to an elderly man who walked down a dark street, one of us yet he seemed broken off, wandering and alone.

I followed her gaze and watched as he slowly move over the old pavements, his mouth moving as if talking to someone who had long gone. Yet all I saw was the shape of an elderly man, no signs of who he was or what he was there for, it was like he was closed to me. As if sensing my thoughts despite my best efforts to guard them, Gabrielle scolding me, whispering.

"No, concentrate," she told me, "Can you sense it?"

I tried once more, and suddenly I did feel something; a sense of loneliness and grief, a feeling of having lost something and of being lost. It hit me hard, flooding my thoughts and I struggled to make sense of the wave of emotions that had entered my thoughts. The strange thing was, I knew they were not mine and a certain part of me felt detached, yet I still felt caught in the strange web that I had made for myself.

"You have to separate yourself from the feelings you read Night, otherwise they may take over and you will feel paralysed to stop them," Gabrielle said, her voice sounding faded as I tried to focus on her voice. Suddenly I felt a jolt as she pulled me back and all the feelings I'd been experiencing quickly stopped. I felt stripped, cold and confused as I looked at her, utterly shocked at what I'd experienced.

"I felt...terrible," I managed to utter the words as gradually I started to feel normal again.

"Yes, the thoughts of the dead can be overpowering at first. When you grow more sensitive to these and learn to keep them at arm's length, you will be able to read them more precisely if you so wish, and without being noticed," she replied, seemingly unconcerned at my hollow state.

"He was so alone, it scared me," I whispered. A look of disgust seemed to grow on Gabrielle's face.

"He is nothing! You cannot have feelings for these creatures; they are black holes in our existence, pointless vacuums that simply take up space."

I looked at her, shocked and silent as she silently stroked the black lace sleeve of her dress. It was as if she had never uttered a word.

"Gabrielle, I don't know what to do..."

"You must protect yourself, your thoughts. Right now you're open to just about anyone who may see you as prey," she told me, coldly.

"I-I don't know how to do that," I responded, perplexed by the word 'prey'. Gabrielle sighed.

"Normally the stronger spirits, such as myself may see useless souls as a way to top up their energy, although you have to be very strong to handle that amount of mass without becoming…wrong. You have to close yourself to spirits that are stronger than you, practice what I have shown you tonight."

With fear I nodded, thinking of Magnus and if he had existed in this seemingly callous way. He had known Gabrielle, although he'd never mentioned her; I wondered why he'd kept her a secret from me.

She laughed a low guttural sound that brought me straight out of her thoughts. Her face now looked bitter and twisted as she stood up from the edge of the roof. I could tell she'd read my thoughts and it displeased her, yet she seemed to take pleasure in the bitterness that flooded her eyes.

"Magnus was one to always make me feel small and insignificant…even though I was far the stronger being than him! Do you know what that is like? Have you ever had the inability to feel safe or as if you could possibly make the slightest of differences? Perhaps you should know what I mean…"

I stepped back upon the ledge, the dying nightlife of London only now becoming apparent to me, clubbers on their way back home often staggering along the old pavements. I could feel the wind violently blowing around me, while in front Gabrielle approached me with an evil grin on her bright red lips.

"When was the last time you felt this small, Night?" I heard her voice but around it came laughter, surrounding me completely yet I was unable to distinguish the voices or where they were coming from. Confused I looked around me, yet saw nothing, only feeling the cold air that blew around my hair.

Panicked I stepped off the ledge and into the just brightening night sky; I knew it would not be long before sunrise.

Suddenly they started to appear out of the air, spirits all around me, closing in on me until all I could see were figures smiling and laughing, all I could hear was their laughter and taunts. The sky seemed to fill with them and I was unable to count their number; it looked like hundreds.

Men and women, teenagers and children crowded around me in a menacing circle and for the first time maybe ever, I felt claustrophobic. What do you want from me, I thought as I felt panic rising inside me. There was nothing I could do to get away, the spirits seeming to drain my energy so that I felt weak and scared.

They felt strong, every single one of them there for Gabrielle's purpose and as these thoughts clouded my mind I struggled around the seemingly growing parade. I knew then that she was controlling them somehow, but who the hell was she to do that? A sense of dread seared through me and I stopped thinking.

I tried to push through them but I grew disorientated, unable to see the way forward and desperately struggling to free myself from their grasps and I realised they were able to hurt me.

I heard Gabrielle in the distance, taunting me, "When was the last time you felt so small, Night, do you feel small now?" Her laughter blended in with the others until it was unable to tell who was laughing.

One large man snatched my arm and gripped me tightly while a young blonde woman pulled at my hair, her bright red nails broken and torn they maniacally tried to scratch me and it was then I screamed.

Perhaps they were insane or for some reason saw me as the enemy but I knew Gabrielle had some sort of strange power over these people. But at the time I couldn't tell what that was.

Although they were all around me I could tell the sun was almost up and I'd be banished once more. As I screamed again and again I felt everything dim around me and I knew their faces would haunt me for more than just one night.

I started to relax when I realised that it would soon all be over and once again I would find myself back in Magnus's room. As I watched their faces slowly fade into black I thought once more of Magnus and his love for me…perhaps he did not want me to know the cruelty of Gabrielle.

And just before the blackout, I heard a woman's angry scream.

Chapter Twelve

I do remember the last time I felt small, insignificant; it was on the way back from Thailand, sitting on a crowded plane with my mother. She found it hard to understand me, why I had changed so much into a withdrawn depressive.

She understood what I'd been through, but part of her just wished I would snap out of it and talk about home-made potato soup or something that connected me to her daughter.

I sat quietly wrapped in a cardigan, watching the beautiful sky of Thailand just disappear beneath me and I felt incredibly sad, yet no tears came. Around my neck I'd tied the charm that I'd took from the beach, and my mother noticed as I absentmindedly twisted it with my fingers.

"Is that something you got over here, love?" She asked, still trying to make conversation. I nodded and she squeezed my hand tightly, a look of sadness coming over her face and I just wished that under all the small talk and niceties that every family had could simply brush away and we could say what we really wanted to say, instead of all the other stuff that got in the way.

The important stuff just got pushed and pushed and pushed behind everything else and it stupidly reminded me of our closet at home, full of junk that nobody wanted and a few valuable memories buried beneath it all to be forgotten until the next spring clean.

On the long plane journey back to London she would stroke my messy hair and remark upon how I refused to cut it before we left when the truth was I was holding onto some memory I loathed to let go of yet.

Sue was my mother's name, now I just think of her as Sue; not that it really matters. Sue looked uncomfortable every inch of that journey, not being used to travel and then there was the small matter of her disturbed daughter with the messy hair.

I remember sitting there on the plane and trying so very hard to make more of an effort with her, to somehow break through the barrier but I ended up just sitting there thinking 'snap out of it, please snap out of it now' but just sitting there motionless and staring at the clouds.

I'd like to say things got better when we arrived back home; of course for the first couple of weeks I did stay at the family home, nurtured and crowded by family and forced to eat food that I no longer wanted. The thing was, whenever I began to relax and enjoy things just for a minute I remembered everything that'd happened and it no longer tasted so good.

And of course people commented on my body, forever changed by my travels but that didn't bother me; at the back of my mind, being thin had always been a good thing, especially with the material I'd been brought up around.

Magazines with covers of skinny models, television presenters, actresses and pop stars all racing to become an impossible size zero. I'd known friends who'd starved for months, calling themselves fat for being unable to fit into a size six.

At home, the one person I'd wanted to hear from had been Alex, and that call happened the day after I returned back home. My return had been reported on the news 'journalist returns from horror trip' but I'd refused a proper interview.

He'd called the same night sounding worried, upset and relieved at the same time; it had taken me back, to get such a reaction from him. I had half been expecting a call from him but for it to be more along the lines of the old days, not…his tears.

He promised to visit me, but that only happened after I had returned to my small apartment, assuring my family that I wouldn't kill myself if left alone. By that time the news had died down and I was given the opportunity to start living a normal life; the publishing deal, my friends and the whole of London awaited me…but all I could think of was him.

I had fallen asleep on the couch; one of the rare times I actually got into a deep, motionless sleep. I awoke to find him there watching me, his gentle touch on my long, unruly hair.

"Night, don't worry it's me," he said softly as I came awake with a start.

"Alex? What are you doing here?" I asked him, perplexed, the moonlight rays bathed the living room with soft light and I saw his familiar face and soft brown hair – shorter than I'd remembered. He smiled at me warmly, but even in the dim light I could see a trace of sadness in his eyes.

"I wanted to see you…it took me a while to get the courage but I'm here now. You left your door open," a note of concern crept into his voice and I remembered the phone call, how upset he'd been. I sat up and gently trace a finger over his mouth, still slightly confused from my dreams. It somehow felt so right that he was there, with me.

"I-I missed you so much," I whispered, as he looked deep into my eyes and I noticed a tear leave his deep blue eye. He nodded, but left the tear.

"I missed you every day…I felt so guilty," he replied, handing me a glass of water that I took gingerly from his hand.

I'd completely lost track of time that night, sleeping erratically and only eating when I remembered to eat. My mum had of course been visiting often, with containers of soup and cooking me breakfasts; if it hadn't been for her I may have lost a very unhealthy amount of weight.

It was surreal with Alex as I stood up and led him to my spotless bedroom, practically unlived in since I'd returned. We lay on the bed together and talked for what seemed like hours, about us and everything we regretted.

It was like all the pain had lifted and suddenly we saw each other without the barrier that had existed in our relationship for so long, perhaps not from the start, but had developed as we grew apart from each other. It had made everything difficult.

As we spoke all that seemed to exist was pure love and a deep understanding, although in my heart I could tell Alex would never forgive himself for what had happened out in Thailand. I never questioned his reasons for coming that night; we never talked about Thailand at all. For the next three days we existed in a kind of bubble, protected from everything around us.

"Do you think things could have been different, if I'd never left?" I asked him jokingly, as we lay together that first night.

"You know they would have been," he said as he pulled me against him and held me tightly. I closed my eyes and realised I felt so safe with him, a feeling I'd longed for ever since the day I'd left him at the airport.

I looked into his eyes, searching for a real answer I asked, "But you know I had to go?"

He shook his head sadly, and it was then he kissed me and it felt like we were melting into one.

All my emotions welled up inside of me and I let them out through him, the only way I really could. Our kiss seemed to last forever and soon we were undressing each other in a familiar way yet surreally it felt new.

His body was the same as I'd always remembered, yet I knew he was older and the past year had changed him considerably; the old Alex was gone and it was almost like exploring a distant lover from a past life.

It was a gift, something I thought I'd never know again; to make love again, our connection somehow stronger than it ever had been before. I gently traced over the familiar marks on his body, the beautiful flaws that made him my Alex.

It was only after a while that I noticed the tears in his eyes, I kissed them away softly and whispered 'you don't have to cry anymore'. He laughed and held me closer, and it was perfect.

We stayed in the apartment, talking and caressing each other, making love and almost pretending that nothing had changed between us, almost as if I had never really left. I didn't want to think about the truth, and probably I knew that it would never last; it was too perfect to be true.

We cooked for each other and he looked after me in a way that made me feel special and closed away from the rest of the world. We watched old DVDs and listened to old music that had been lying around my apartment from years back and most of all we just talked about everything and nothing.

At one point it felt like it would last forever; I never wanted him to leave but he had a life in London and I couldn't expect to take him away from it, to spend eternity in our bubble.

I stood at the door and watched him go, feeling a hollow ache deep in my heart. I couldn't know what would happen next, could never have known that, but something felt wrong.

It was like I wanted to stop time from moving, to pull him back in with me and just hold him, but he smiled at me and the feeling was quickly gone; a ghost in my mind.

Then I began to write. I stared out the window for what seemed like an hour before walking over to my PC, turning it on and actually writing for the first time since I returned back to London.

What came out of me was the same story from the island, dark and haunted. I wrote for the rest of the day, completely enveloped in my own fictional world until the early hours of the night when exhaustion finally set in.

I slept without waking once, yet my dreams were odd and broken…yet there was something closed off to me.

Why had I let Alex leave and why did I not hear from him afterwards? As I sat in the warm darkness of Magnus's apartment I tried to remember what had happened to me, why Alex had not returned to the apartment.

I felt cold as I began to really remember the night of my death: it had been only a few days after Alex had left, yet I'd spiralled down into my own little dark world. I had been writing almost non-stop, a dark story pouring out of me as I frantically typed the keys.

I had been sleeping when I heard the noise that woke me, and in the darkness I slowly rose from the sofa that I'd resorted to sleeping on. The noise came from the hall, and as my eyes adjusted I realised there was an intruder in the apartment.

The dark figure had knocked me to the ground and my body felt cold as the sharp steel blade entered my stomach. He stabbed me again in the chest and as I lay bleeding I looked up to see that the figure was searching for something.

The memory flashed into my mind like lightning as I remembered him turning towards me; it had been Petri who had broke into my apartment!

But something didn't make sense; as I looked at him a thought entered my head: 'Amon'. Perhaps my mind was confused, irrational as pain spread through my body but as I lay dying I somehow knew Amon was my killer. Yet how could that be true?

Petri's face yet…somehow it wasn't the Petri who had saved me that night on the island. Another memory flash, this time it was Amon and Petri sitting around the fire. I tried to picture the chanting, the strange ritual, the confused look on Amon's face before the fired shots…could it be possible that Amon had swapped bodies with Petri just before he died?

None of it made sense, yet the more I thought about it the more it became plausible that Amon had swapped bodies with Petri and for some reason followed me to London. But then there was another question: why follow me?

I had given evidence that Petri had saved my life, believing that Amon had died so what reason would Amon have for killing me, apart from maybe a strong hatred for journalists.

Then I remembered the ritual, the charm he'd held over the blazing fire as he chanted desperately. I remembered returning to the island, taking my notes and finding that same charm, putting it in my pocket.

When I returned to London I had placed it in a box under my bed, trying to forget the memories until one day when I could look at its contents and feel detached enough to wonder what drove me to stay in Thailand, to visit the island.

A chill spread through me at this thought; was it possible that Amon had followed me to retrieve his charm? If he was able to body swap – something I'd never thought possible – then somehow he needed the charm to be able to perform such a ritual. And if that was the case, the charm was his way of being immortal, living forever by jumping from body to body.

Yet surely what I was thinking was impossible, that somehow a spell or curse could bestow such power on an object that it would allow the user to swap bodies. I sat coldly thinking, still shy from the memories that I'd forced to enter my mind.

Reliving my death had been painful, remembering the coldness of the blade and the smell of my own blood as I lay on the floor dying. I felt a great anger towards Amon or Petri, whoever had taken away my life so cruelly.

I closed the memories out, overwhelmed by the emotions that somehow become much more powerful than I can handle in death. I decided I need not know of these things, so what if the crazy feelings were true and Amon was still out there? It could not affect me, I was not after all looking for some anger-fuelled vengeance like Gabrielle, overtaken by power and greed.

Perhaps Gabrielle, with all her wisdom could give me answers to my questions, but first there was someone else I needed to see, even if it was just one last time.

The memories were still there, of him holding me and loving me, his beautiful eyes and strong smile.

I pushed away all thoughts of the island and the ritual; it never even occurred to me whether Amon had found the necklace I kept in my room

Chapter Thirteen

Early the next evening I quietly entered Alex's flat on the second floor of his apartment block. It was already very dark outside and the flat was dimly lit, with one room shining brighter than all the rest.

In anticipation I took a deep breath as I moved closer to the light and gently passed between the slightly open door. I didn't know what to expect after what seemed like an eternity of selfish thoughts this side of the dark, of blocking out our past that we shared for so long with one another. It hurt me to think that I had willingly done this when what we'd had was so special but perhaps we souls get lost, torn from our previous lives and unable to find our way. Maybe that was why I seemed stuck.

I stupidly thought he might have got on with his own life, taking his photographs and going out for drinks with the same annoying crowd that I never felt a part of when we were together. Whatever I was expecting, it hadn't been anywhere near what I saw that night, and it surprised me.

Alex sat slouched by his desk, a lamp shining brightly overhead. He looked scruffier than usual as I approached the desk where he silently worked.

He wore an old blue t-shirt that he'd had ever since I'd known him and brown combat trousers with a tear in the left leg. I could tell he'd been awake for hours and probably hadn't had a good night's sleep in days.

He was mainly a photojournalist and I saw he was looking at newspaper cuttings; not unusual for Alex to save his work although I'd never known him to study them so carefully before.

But when I looked closely I realised he was unshaven; he looked tired and sad as he moved the cuttings around the table.

I detected a hint of frustration in his emotions and when I looked at the cuttings I saw why.

The stories he was looking at were about me; my 'nightmare' holiday in Thailand and more recently, my murder. It pained me to look at those stories, reminders of my death I did not need or want to look upon.

The killer was still said to be unknown and I knew right away, by the look on his face that Alex was trying to somehow find my killer. He was staring intently at my death, as if he had missed something, some vital clue that would somehow make everything okay.

It was a shock to see him like that; pale and thin I could tell he had not been eating properly. All the time I had been in this state I never really stopped to think of how my death would have affected those I once loved…so selfish of me to carry on the way I did, forgetting my past and memories which were too painful to carry around with my spiritual body.

Now it hit me just what he must have been going through after what happened, that he did still love me. I wanted to cry, to scream at him to see me, to hear me but I felt so weak against the build-up of emotions that was slowly taking over me.

He didn't even look up as I tried to pick up his nearby glass and failed. I wanted to spill the remains of his water over the newspaper, to tell him to leave it alone, to stay out of things that he did not understand.

Instead I circled the table in thought and concentration, took in a deep breath and said, "Alex, listen to me."

He did nothing in response, no sign that he had heard what I'd said even though to me I had spoken as clear as day. Slowly growing agitated I tried again, louder this time. I started to circle the table faster, created a slight breeze around him that I hoped he would notice, one of the cuttings falling to the floor.

"Alex, it's me, Night! Please, I want you to hear me!" I realised that this was obviously useless and a waste of my time, as I continued trying to affect the air around me.

But as he picked up the glass of water and sipped his face seemed to change and he looked up at the spot I now stood, trying to move the cuttings around his table in frustration.

His eyes looked cold and unfeeling, as if he had blocked out the recent pain and was staring into a blank space. For a few seconds he did not move and at first I thought he had seen something, or perhaps noticed a changed in the air.

I wanted him to sense me so badly that I began to think that he knew, somehow he knew I was there. It wasn't true though, he continued to stare for a moment longer before slamming down his glass and walking into the sitting room, where he sat alone.

I followed him, unable to make myself known although for the past couple of hours I really tried, once managing to knock over a dish-towel in the kitchen.

Alex paid no attention and before long I just watched him until he drifted off to sleep, still wearing the same grubby clothes on the old sofa that he'd had since he'd first moved in.

I felt a deep sadness, unable to connect with Alex when I could tell he was alone in his heart. Feeling helpless, I moved back to the desk in the other room to study the cuttings based on my death.

I smiled at the notebook that lay to the left of the table; his notes had always been a mess but due to long-term practice they read to me clearly. My smile soon faded when I saw exactly what he had been writing.

Clever Alex, he had matched the Thai murders to my death in London but what worried me was that he hadn't stopped there.

"Alex, my dear what trouble are you getting into now?" I whispered to myself as I continued to read through his scribbling, searching in horror for some sense of his actions.

Whoever it was had obviously disappeared into the background after my murder, the fact that my apartment had been raided but nothing obvious taken had raised suspicion.

That was natural and just reinforced my memories of laying there watching Petri as he maniacally upturned the rooms around me, my consciousness fading into black.

His notes grew more confusing as I read on, unable to make sense of some of his ramblings but what became clear over time was that he intended to trace my killer and was getting close to two members of an underground Thai community here in London in the hope that they will lead him to the truth.

Alarm bells started ringing in my mind and I felt a surge of anger, like electricity shoot through me. He had no right, my death was nothing to do with him! Without hesitation I knew he was going to get himself into some kind of trouble that he'd be unable to avoid. I had an urge to take the cuttings, the notebook and leave but I stopped myself, stepping back from my feelings until sadness flooded through me like cold dark water.

The fact was, I hoped he would never know what had happened, that he would go back to taking pictures of politicians and parties.

"Oh lover, if only you knew the truth..." I muttered, thinking that Petri or Amon had probably left London by that time. I failed to take into account the importance of what he'd been looking for.

As the night grew colder I felt a deep sorrow for my ex, the love I'd long left behind. I found myself wishing that he would only leave the past alone, to stay out of the things that he could never understand and move on with his own life. After all, it was a precious gift, one that is forever taken for granted.

Once again entering the sitting room I sat on the floor in front of his sleeping figure, one arm draped over the arm of the sofa. The rain fell heavily upon the window yet he slept soundly as I watched him with sorrow in my heart. I felt an urge to protect him and for a moment I had a horrible flash, a thought that Gabrielle may have followed me there.

Gabrielle, with her loveless unfeeling hatred, would she dare harm him? I was scared of her, I knew that but a part of me also felt she would do me no harm for if she had wanted that she could have done so a long time ago.

There was no intrusion; we were alone. It seemed there was nothing I could do to reach him, and almost resigned by the fact I made up my mind to leave him be soon, my old love.

I tried to touch him but as usual my touch went right through him, my arm shaking with concentration. Finally, softly, I ran my finger through his hair; it was longer than usual, also scruffy.

I was surprised when I felt how soft his hair was, something I'd forgotten long ago and slowly he stirred, as if aware of the movement. I moved back, taken by surprise as he woke to look right through me.

Turning over he sleepily opened his eyes and I smiled then, the colours in them still as bright as ever. He looked tired as hell and I felt sorry for disturbing him, but as I took in his sight one last time before leaving him for good, I saw something which turned me cold.

As he moved, the necklace hidden by his t-shirt became more visible and I saw those familiar dark and wooden shapes; with horror I instantly recognised it as the charm from the beach.

Chapter Fourteen

Alex was in danger and needed my help; my senses told me that Amon was still searching for the ritual necklace but I knew not of his whereabouts.

In a panic I felt helpless to protect my ex, to somehow stop him from searching for my killer. What if Amon found him first? It was too terrifying to think about and I knew I needed help…but something stopped me from going to Gabrielle; she was after all against interfering with the 'living world'.

I decided I had to try and communicate with the living, to somehow get a warning to Alex no matter how it sounded. But this was a big step for me, something I would never have dreamt of doing before; cowering in the shadows and forgetting my past.

My fear and ongoing love for Alex forced me to search for answers, to protect him from the things I had exposed him to and I knew that if he died I would never forgive myself.

I thought of Alex who wore the leather knotted necklace with the dirty wooden charms in the hope it would bring him closer to me, blissfully unaware that he was probably attracting an evil force to him like a magnet. Of course I couldn't possibly know that, but I had a feeling that did not bode well and it made me even more determined to somehow make contact.

The next night I left the place I came to know as Magnus's room, the room I always returned to when night fell over the stars. Another mystery that I may never know, shrouded from me by a thin veil of knowledge. If only I still had my teacher to guide me, to tell me what these things meant.

I was above the city, listening to the noise of London life; every voice, every thought blended in together as carefully I listened, searching. I breezed through the air, cloaked and confident in my movements, until at last I found what I was vaguely looking for and suddenly I looked up to find myself in a small dark room.

Four people sat before a round table, the focal point a middle-aged woman who seemed to have an energy that was more vibrant than the others. She was dressed in a long woollen knit jumper that draped around her, and a long skirt that made her look demur.

Her face was lined with small wrinkles and her hair was a soft white-yellow colour, shoulder length. Her green eyes looked old and misty, unsmiling.

Around her sat two women and a man, all of whom had an air of tension and in the man, a slight trepidation. In the middle of the table sat a clear glass tumbler and I realised they meant to perform a séance. Letters were carved onto the mahogany table and I realised the table was in fact a Ouija board.

The elderly lady was talking although to me she sounded very quiet, as if somebody had turned down the volume control. I realised a protection spell had been cast to guard from evil, but I moved forward anyway and touched the glass.

Everybody at the table jumped, although the glass settled back into place without tumbling over. The women was talking again, they all held hands tightly and suddenly I heard her voice clearly, as if I had suddenly come out of a warp.

"If there are any spirits here, please make yourselves known," she spoke with a tremble in her voice, possibly out of old age or fear. She spoke again.

"If there are any spirits listening, please tap or knock the glass," her voice was louder this time.

I moved around the table, watching them and feeling completely out of my comfort zone. Reaching out to the wall, I tapped once. The two women reacted by looking around the table and almost jumping out of their seats.

"Yes, I can sense you," the woman continued, "if you are still there then please tap again, twice."

I tapped the wall twice, as she had asked but all of a sudden I went cold. The women twitched and her expression seemed to change.

"Damien, is that you? I told you not to come back here, Damien," she said, her words confusing me as I looked around the empty room.

In the corner stood a young black man, with skin almost the colour of ash and very short black hair. He wore a light blue denim shirt and dark jeans, a menacing smile on his face.

He ignored me as I glanced at him nervously. I moved towards the woman who seemed not to notice me, into her ear I tried to talk.

"I am Night, I need your help, please," I told her, and I realised that she had heard something.

She shifted her weight in the chair and looked uncomfortable, before asking, "Who is that? What do you want?"

"I need your help, my name is Night," I said, feeling more distressed at the look of the man in the corner, "Please, someone is in danger and needs your help."

I was interrupted as the man suddenly seemed to snap into life, charging at the table and making everyone around it jump out of their seats as the table was pushed forward, barely missing the elderly host.

The woman seemed to lapse into a terrible frenzy of chants, her wrinkled hands shaking I felt her words grow quieter as I watched the others around the table, their faces confusing and frightened.

The table settled back to normal, the angry spirit gone as slowly the host sat back in her chair, looking as if she had never left her spot at the head of the table. Slowly, one of the women sat down in imitation of her host, followed by the gentleman. The third women, perhaps mid-forties muttered that she had to leave; she looked shaken as she walked out of the door.

I felt anger rise up inside me, and sparked by their ignorance I knocked over the glass on the table. The woman screamed and the man placed the glass upright again, his hand shaking slightly.

I moved around, touching the back of the man's head and making him jump, although he said nothing.

The host moved her chair closer to the table and signalled for the others to do the same, before speaking.

"Now, let us all put our hands on the glass for the séance," she said, talking loudly again.

"Please, is the young lady still there? I sense a lot of emotion, tell me, do you wish us harm?"

I moved back towards the glass and conjured up the strength to move the glass towards 'no'. The female guest looked at the well-dressed man in response, her eyes shifting from his to the woman's.

"Did you feel that?" She whispered, her fear showing on her face. The man quietly shook his head, and waiting for the next question.

"Could you tell us your name?" The host asked, ignoring her guests as if in a deep concentration.

I once again moved the glass, at first unsure of what to do but then sliding over to 'n' then 'i' until I had spelled out 'Night'. They waited for a couple of minutes in silence, until the elderly woman once again spoke up.

"Night? That is not your name, surely?"

Feeling frustrated, I moved the glass harshly to 'yes', causing the two guests to jump back in fright. They looked at each other nervously, before glancing at the host who nodded for them to continue.

I didn't give them a chance to place their hands back on the glass tumbler, before moving it to spell out my own message, leaving gaps between the words. The man and women looked shocked, their eyes never leaving the glass while the host looked on speechless, an eyebrow raised at my energy.

I spelt out 'I need help. Alex is in danger.' There was silence for a while, before the woman stood up at the table and motioned her guests to leave.

"I'm sorry, I cannot continue with this session," she told them, "I hope you are happy with the results."

After little protests, the guests did leave while I paced the floors feeling more and more agitated. As the guests left the room, the woman moved over to a dark wood cabinet in the corner and took out a small crystal glass, into which she poured neat brandy and sipped carefully. When we were finally alone she sat down, composed as ever and looking warily to both sides of her vision.

There was something, or someone she was scared of and I had seen him, menacing and stubborn; I thought I could still feel his presence near me, but if he was here he had hidden himself. I thought 'curiosity killed the cat', which seemed to please him.

"Night, who is this person?" She spoke slowly and clearly, and I moved quickly until I was standing right next to her. She knew I was there, but her eyes did not show any sign of fear; she looked deadly serious.

I was amazed to have this feeling, to be able to communicate with the living so effectively, that this woman could maybe even hear me as she appeared to do earlier.

I began to speak, but was interrupted when a man's terrible scream filled the whole room; it was 'Damien'. I turned to look as his head seemed to stretch high on his neck, his mouth twisted in the scream.

His arms appeared to be disjointed and moving in ways that weren't natural and his shirt was badly ripped, but the scream itself caused me to recoil in horror. The woman heard it too and began to recast her protection, talking quickly and loudly while covering her ears and crouching down low.

The worst part was his eyes: blood seemed to running down them as if he was crying thick and heavy tears of dark red. He seemed to be convulsing on the spot, as if dying in an agonising, painful way but there was something else that puzzled me.

He seemed to be putting on a show for my benefit, as if to ward me away from the frail-looking woman. It was almost as if she was his possession and this gruesome act was a way to frighten away other spirits. He seemed to want to frighten her too, and I wondered what connection this 'Damien' could have.

The next part happened very fast; I heard the odd word, 'be gone' and 'away' and then, very powerfully I was cast out of the room as if pushed by an invisible barrier, expanding until I was out on the streets.

It was busy and people rushed around me, through me completely unaware of my presence; I was after all, but a ghost, back to normal.

The ghost, 'Damien' had ruined my chance to communicate my message; I felt his anger loud and clear and it shocked me. I realised it might be a battle to get my message through, but it was necessary to save Alex; to let him know I was there and to stop him from chasing Amon.

I was shaken, confused and no further towards reaching Alex, but I knew I had to try somehow. My energy slowly began to replenish, my spiritual body felt weak from the things I'd achieved with the psychic.

It was in a way, a revelation; I could contact the living and affect them, I could change things if I really tried. It was strange to think that I'd ignored this kind of spiritual activity when I was alive, and now to find out it was true…it opened doors that I'd believed could be closed forever.

Now I was determined and sure of myself; there was a way I could achieve my goal and soon it was all I could manage to care about, lost in the horror of my past life and fear for my one-time love.

I realised there were plenty of so-called 'psychics' out there, I just had to find the right one, at the right time.

My next trip led me to the basement of an old museum in the West End of London, where I was confused to find camera crews and darkness. I'd sensed the presence of mediums, but I could not have predicted the attitude of the people I met there.

I could see three men and two women filming for a television show that investigated ghost hunts, but nevertheless at least one of the men generated a certain psychic ability with his energy almost pulling me towards him like a magnet. I could not help but feel I had to communicate with this man.

The show was so obviously filmed with the lights out for extra effect, although it confused me why they would so desperately provoke what they did not understand for the benefit of viewers at home.

The building was an old Victorian style, the perfect place for a TV crew to investigate its recent 'hauntings'. Old paintings hung on the wall, mostly portraits with faces that stared with almost intelligent eyes.

One of the women, a presenter called Marie was leading the others through the lower rooms of the basement and reporting a drop in the temperature, and carefully I looked in the shadows; so far there was nothing, no spirits. I knew then it was my chance.

She had long dark hair pulled back in a pony tail and was fairly young, about my age when I died. From what I could tell she hadn't experienced much real activity on the spiritual side so I focused my attentions on the man that I'd first noticed, a psychic by the name of Nick.

He wore a thick velvet jacket over an embroidered white shirt and plain black trousers, wrapped up in a scarf he looked around making comments about the history of the building and the feelings he was sensing around it.

It was only when I moved up close that I saw a change in him; he'd sensed my presence. He had stiffened, listening carefully but eventually deciding to move on with the rest of the crew, only after a few minutes of my deliberate attention did he speak out loud.

"Okay," he said, "someone's in the room with us."

Two of the men moved forward, the presenter Marie followed towards Nick.

"Nick, are you alright?" I heard a voice ask him, he nodded before replying.

"Yes, I just felt a deliberate temperature drop around me but I'll be okay. Does anyone else feel anything?" He asked.

The other woman nodded her head, "Yeah I think so, but it might just be my imagination. Is anyone there?"

"If anyone is there, please tap or make a noise," Marie spoke up loudly. I tapped the hard stone wall twice as loudly as I could right next to Nick, who jumped slightly. The others looked around as if almost in a panic.

"Oh God, did you catch that on film, Dave?" asked one of the men. Everyone agreed they'd heard the tap. Marie stepped into the middle of the small crowd and spoke again.

"If you are here with us now, tap twice please," she said.

I tapped twice on the wall, although now it was more of an effort for me; I reminded myself to conserve my energy for when I really needed it. Then I remembered I had a whole room full of it...

I took a moment to compose myself before thrusting toward one of the camera men and quickly feeding on his energy, allowing him to feel the air as I moved around him. He looked around, frightened but unaware of the small amount of energy I'd sapped from him.

"I think I just felt something," he said. A couple of them turned to him and asked what was wrong, to which he replied, "I dunno, I'm sure there's something following me."

Nick said, "There is definitely more than one spirit here tonight, but where they are I can't tell, they're probably cloaked."

"What about that tapping, Nick?" Marie asked.

"I think it's a female, I can sense her presence and she's upset about something. I'm not sure of her name but I'm just getting random words in my head."

So he knew I was there. Good, I thought as I watched them make their way towards the stairs. As for other spirits, I wasn't aware of them down in the basement but I couldn't afford for them to interfere this time.

I realised I had to make a noise in the basement quick, and searching around I saw the perfect thing; an old vase. With force I knocked it to the ground, causing it to shatter and the noise to reverberate all around the room.

The two women screamed and two of the men came running to the spot, desperately searching with their flashlights to locate the source of the noise. One of them picked up a shard, before shouting at the others to stay back.

"Guys, it looks like some sort of ornament or vase, stay back it's all over the floor!"

Marie looked concerned, before asking, "Is that still her? Should I ask her what she wants?"

Nick nodded, but reminded her to be careful not to 'upset' me. He should've known I was already 'upset'. I kicked one of the vase shards across the floor, hitting the other woman's shoe and causing her to cry out again.

"Sorry, something just touched my shoe!"

"Okay, if you can hear us, if you're still there please tap twice," Marie shouted loudly. I tapped back quickly, eager to get through to the crew.

"Good, thank you," Marie replied, "Do you mean us any harm tonight? Tap once for no and twice for yes."

Yes, I would mean them harm if they took any longer, I thought to myself before tapping once. Marie let out a theatrical sigh of relief for the cameras before continuing her attempt to communicate.

"Do you have a message for us?"

Again, I tapped but twice this time. This seemed to be a signal for them to carry on upstairs where they had set out a Ouija board, but I had almost run out of patience.

I moved quickly towards Nick again, touching the back of his neck and making him shiver. I tried to talk to him, first by saying his name.

He seemed to hear me, while one of the cameramen reported seeing a shadow at the top of the stairs. Everyone climbed up to that spot while I ignored them, concentrating on the psychic.

"Nick, you have to listen to me, please I need your help," I said, trying to get through to him as clearly as possible, "Someone is in danger". Slowly he nodded, unsure of my words and wary of the camera team.

"Look guys, she's trying to talk to me...that is not very usual for a spirit, believe me. She's actually talking to me directly, she says someone's in danger, I'm not sure who exactly that is," Nick shouted to the crew, before following them up the stone stairs and fastening the buttons on his jacket.

"What, one of us is in danger?" Asked the woman with the blonde hair, before turning to Marie for confirmation.

"Can you ask her; is it one of us Nick?" Marie asked, her voice slightly more raised and unsure of her environment. Nick nodded.

"Please, whoever you are, are you trying to tell us one of us is in danger?" Nick asked quietly, his eyes shut in concentration.

"No, for God's sake listen to me!" I shouted as anger built up inside me, the crew now stood around the reception table, focused on Nick as he put one hand over his ear in grimace, "It's someone I used to know, he's important to me so please I need you to help him, to tell him he's in danger and to stop what he's doing!"

I was shouting at him, suddenly again so angry at the people who were filming the show, and Nick for not being able to understand me. I was moving around him in flashes, uncloaked and I could tell he was seeing shapes as I darted around still raising my voice.

Marie asked, "Nick, are you alright?"

He nodded in response before replying, "Yeah...I'm getting a lot of words through at the moment, I can tell she's very upset and there's something important to her that she wants to say," he looked up before continuing, "I can honestly say this hardly ever happens to me, I don't quite know what to make of it."

Nick slumped into a chair, looking weak and dazed, a hand over his head. One of the men knelt down to try and reassure him.

"I'm not feeling too good, she just flew at me...I'm not comfortable with continuing do you mind if I leave the room please," Nick said slowly and quietly, carefully trying to recover from my strange tirade.

Although I had put him through discomfort, he did not attempt to banish me or protect himself even once. I watched silently as the crew crowded around him, making sure that he was okay to continue but still he indicated that he'd like to leave the room.

I followed him in the darkness, through corridors with thick red carpets, always looking through the light of his flashlight. I felt protective of Nick, although I'd given up trying to communicate with him.

I think he was aware of me watching him but for the next ten minutes I kept quiet, observing his behaviour until I grew aware of another female presence in the room. She too was a spirit, her long red hair wet and falling around her face.

Suddenly she sprinted towards me, her long white gown trailing mud and dirty autumn leaves, before disappearing for good.

Nick waited, watching the space where she had passed through, before finding a nearby couch and sitting quietly with his head in his hands.

I sat down beside him, trying to think of what to do next and failing. I was so obviously inexperienced and clumsy, a ghost with a bad temper and even worse communicative skills, but I had tried.

"I know you're still there," Nick said quietly, making me jump for once. Slowly he turned his head to the direction I was sitting in, seeming to look both at me and right through me at the same time.

"I'm sorry but I can't help you. Please leave here, Night," he said, his words chilling me. I continued to stare at him, unsure whether he could see me. Either way, he knew I was there and I felt I had to comply with his wishes.

Frustrated and appalled, I exited the museum leaving Nick and his company behind. By this time my need and desperation had calmed somewhat, aware that Alex was still in danger, but perhaps not immediate danger.

Unsure of what to do next, I decided I had to plan my meetings a little more carefully than I'd first thought.

Chapter Fifteen

David Whiteman was a psychic who wrote for the London Trinity where he claimed to reply to readers' questions by communicating with the dead. For example if OAP Francis, aged 88 wrote in to ask about her dearly departed husband of ten years, he would kindly write back to say that her husband was in a good place and that her missing necklace was in the bottom drawer of her lucky oak wood cabinet.

He made his money exploiting his contact with the dead, although how honestly he replied to readers queries was always in question. His advice was always kind, his outlook always sunny and every spirit replied in what seemed to be a good mood. It gave off a somewhat rosy approach to spirit contact where he left out anything undesirable – mostly probably because he would be out of a job otherwise.

As I watched him move around his house, where he lived alone I tried to make up my mind how to approach him. I debated for close enough to twenty minutes, finding his bedtime ritual oddly relaxing before I made my decision and although I had built up my strength, my hopes were nevertheless dampened from the previous night's disaster.

He was what I'd call 'tubby' as he plodded around his bedroom, short brown greying hair receding slightly on the top of his head. His eyes were brown and friendly, his skin fairly pale although nothing compared to Gabrielle.

Wearing pyjamas he slowly walked into his en-suite bathroom where he removed his contact lenses and proceeded to find his toothbrush. I followed him into the room and watched as he brushed facing the mirror of his bathroom cabinet.

As he looked into the corner to see my face staring back at him in the mirror, however blurry it may have looked, he almost dropped his toothbrush in shock. Turning around quickly he saw nothing in the brightly lit, white bathroom that he'd tiled himself, before turning back to the mirror.

"Who are you, what do you want?" He asked, voice trembling slightly in an almost sweet sort of way that let me know he was really quite frightened.

"I am Night," I said as I moved out of his sight line, once again hiding myself from his view. Nevertheless he shivered as he felt the cold air move around him, and jumped when I placed a deliberately icy hand on his shoulder.

"Is that...your name?" He asked, making me smile and tut audibly. His short-sighted eyes searched the room as if trying to see me and I was impressed when he turned to the spot where I stood against the sink. Being a journalist myself, I'd always been curious as to David's truthfulness but then, we'd only ever met once before at the London Trinity's Christmas party.

I'd been invited when earlier that year I'd written two pieces on travel for the Trinity, earning a very decent payment for my work. He had been dressed smartly with an attractive woman by his side and a shot of brandy in his hand. He'd nodded politely and excused himself when any interest was shown in his work, preferring not to discuss work matters on personal time.

He gave the impression of someone very private, yet I'd always sensed that something was not quite right. Now looking at him from the other side of things, I could tell he knew I was there and that he could hear me.

Whether or not he recognised the name, I couldn't tell but I could see something flicker in his eyes as he asked the next question.

"What do you want?" He asked, almost in agitation at my presence now.

"I need to ask you for help, David," I told him, speaking slowly and deliberately so to make sure he heard every word, almost enjoying the look on his face, "There is a friend of mine who is in danger; I want you to send a message to him. Do you understand?"

He seemed to hesitate before making his mind up, before storming out of the room. I followed, confused at his reaction to this very simple request. I could tell he felt my presence in his room as he looked into the mirror, searching again to see my face.

"Please, leave me alone, I don't understand you," his voice shocked me, but I listened to what he had to say, "There is nothing you can do for you here, please leave."

I could tell I'd spooked him, and that my presence in his house was an unwelcome one. But why would he panic in such a way? Determined for his help, I refused to leave until I at least had answered. I felt power over him, however wrong that may be I admit I enjoyed the interaction between us while it lasted.

I moved quickly to the mirror and his body stiffened in horror as he watched me dart across the room and shoot through him. Next I knocked over a bottle of aftershave as he crouched down in fright on the floor.

"You know who I am, don't you?" I asked him, my voice deliberately loud so he could not avoid it. I viewed him with pure contempt, annoyed at his will to ignore my pleas.

"You've met me before. You remember my name, don't you?" I asked, my voice filled with spite. Before he could answer, I moved with fury towards the mirror so that he could feel it, causing him to shout out.

"Okay! Okay, let me try to help you!" He cried before I could do any more damage and looking down at him I almost felt sorry for causing him fear. But before I could speak to him, to make my request I saw her; Gabrielle.

She stormed into the room with an anger I had never seen painted deep on her face, her raging heat filled the room. I was frozen to the spot as she shot towards me, her black dress now ripped and trailing across the floor, her red lipstick smeared over her face.

"What in hell do you think you're doing?! I have warned you, never to interfere with life you fool!" Her voice was deep with rage and I realised quickly the full extent of her power, her energy practically took up the whole room.

Her eyes were livid, dark and painted with hatred, her fingernails broken and twisted the colour of fire engine red. Her energy was menacing, almost like electricity moving erratically around us as if ready to strike at any moment.

David was now curled up on the floor, hands over his ears and he screamed when Gabrielle smashed the dressing table mirror. She turned her attention back to me and at once I knew what she intended to do; drain me, teach me a lesson so that I could no longer create stirrings within the world of the living.

A smile of evil appeared on her twisted face, her teeth white and carnivorous as she moved closer to me; I felt unable to move before the truth sunk in and I immediately knew I must leave the house.

I charged out of the side wall, moving through the air without a care for where I was headed, trying to escape from those teeth; that smile. I was in sheer terror as the energy around me felt almost alive. I could feel movement around me, but as I darted around I saw nothing. She was too powerful, too fast and I could hear her screams closing in behind me.

In fear and panic I fled for what felt like whole minutes, terrified of the mass of rage that was Gabrielle. I felt helpless as I thrust through the starless sky, wishing for Magnus to rescue me as her screams turned to cruel laughter behind me.

It seemed like they went on forever, taunting me as if to discard my attempts of escape, but soon enough they faded into the wind and I was left wondering, too afraid to slow down to check if she had gone. I felt a tender darkness deep within me, almost a wicked insanity at the hands of Gabrielle yet I knew she was far stronger than anything I'd ever witnessed; perhaps even Magnus.

Terrified that every spirit I met was one of Gabrielle's henchmen to come and capture me, drain me or attack me I moved higher into the sky. I saw no-one for miles as shakily I tried to calm myself.

I felt amazingly strong as my spirit body blew in the wind, almost feeling at times like I would blow apart completely. Although what I'd been through had been awful, I felt quite peaceful among the darkened clouds. It was exhilarating, although I was nowhere closer to finding a way of helping Alex, which filled me with an inner despair.

I smiled at the wonder of Gabrielle and although she scared me, I would try not to let it show. After all if she meant to destroy me she had the power to do so already in her hands and would have done so by now.

It was 11:45pm, hours until daybreak and I finally chose a building to rest in. That building turned out to be the Centaur Library, a small Edwardian building that attracted me with its architecture and sculptures.

In the darkness I saw at once that the upper floors were filled with many small rooms, all of which were adorned with old books. I ran my fingers through the dust, enjoying the look of the particles in the darkness; yet another odd thing I was able to appreciate on this side of the dark. Each particle shimmered in the darkness, almost as if coming to life – tiny fireflies that shifted in the air around me.

The old books were filled with history of life; I could imagine just how many people had touched them, flicking through the aged paper and savouring the words.

I reasoned with myself over Gabrielle, to think that I could be so terrified by another woman's foul moods. I smiled at the thought that perhaps she had died with PMT, but knew deep down she was probably still close by.

The library became my temporary sanctuary, and I settled down in one of the over-sized antique wooden desks to read about the French Revolution, enjoying the tranquillity that it brought to me.

However, after a while I grew curious to explore the other rooms and found it almost like a maze to navigate around the building. Everything was silent around me, so I was stopped in my tracks when I noticed the dim light illuminating one of the back rooms.

It was strange how I hadn't felt the presence of another soul, yet the light seemed to shine in a way that implied someone was still in the library, a nocturnal occupant.

Carefully, I moved towards the room and the light source with the feeling that I was not alone, hoping it was not another cruel trick from Gabrielle. Her haunting expression lingered in my thoughts, making me want to shiver in an unnatural way.

I was relieved but also worried when I saw that in fact, the library indeed held one living occupant; a male with dark curly hair. He had his back to me, leant over the desk in study and as I watched him in silence I realised he intrigued me enough to stay.

I moved in for a closer look, the lamp on the desk being the only source of light. He continued to write, blatantly unaware that he had company he looked comfortable in his surroundings. I was careful not to 'touch' any objects that stood in the cluttered and dusty room, afraid of startling my new fixation.

I got as close as I dared to at the side of his desk, and when he looked up again at his screen I was able to see his face. He struck me straight away as attractive, his smooth pale skin well-lit under the yellowness of the lamp. He wore black framed glasses and under those, I noticed that he had brilliant blue eyes. I watched those eyes trace the words on the screen of his laptop, the brightness turned down low to make it easy for him to concentrate.

I wondered to myself what this living dweller of darkness was doing in the library at that particular time of night, before I spotted his I.D card; Leon Cardew, senior librarian.

The card showed he was thirty one, a surprising age for someone who looked more like twenty five, yet age mattered not.

There was something I found most curious about his mannerisms as he typed lightly on the keys with long delicate fingers, occasionally checking the notes that lay before him on the desk. And what notes they were, beautiful flowing letters carved in a deep black ink, every one of them slanting to the right in a sort of tranquillity that I wished to possess.

His long-ish curls fell slightly over his forehead without a hint of gel and I couldn't help but think to myself that they must feel soft. I want to touch him badly, but never before in death had I been so indescribably attracted to a member of the living.

I couldn't find an explanation for my behaviour as at first I stood and then sat across from him at the desk, transfixed at this beautiful being. And he was beautiful; there was no doubt about it. Even his sleep deprived eyes had a subtle softness and velocity about them, like giant pools of light blue. For a second I thought about the beautiful clear waters of Thailand; a distant memory.

I sat across the desk for around thirty minutes, just watching him as he stared at the laptop and only occasionally looking over to a spot in the distance. I'd wait for those looks, although I knew he could never possibly see me. I began to feel comfortable in the presence of Leon.

He began to look tired, rubbing those blue eyes underneath the glasses and I once again wondered what he was doing alone for so long. It looked like some sort of study, although I couldn't tell what point or subject of study Mr PhD was trying to get across. It was obviously important, or why stay up in a dark library attracting evil ghosts? And jokes aside, did I see myself as evil? Most probably I did, and perhaps still do. Evil is after all a human trait although not quite human anymore, I lacked a sense of restriction.

Growing bored I slowly paced around the room, perusing the book covers and waiting to see how long he would stay. When I moved from the desk I noticed a slight pause in Leon's typing, a sign perhaps that he had detected a change in the air, before he began typing again.

He had continued to type ever since, giving no sign that he sensed my presence so when I purposefully – and silently - moved a book and accidentally knocked some papers to the floor I was surprised at his reaction.

"What do you want from me?" He asked, a tone of trepidation in his voice as he looked at the spot where the papers had fallen. It broke the silence of the room almost violently as I stood silently, unmoving and unsure of what to do, how was it that he had sensed me? I waited in shock and a small hint of fear, trying to predict his next move.

He waited, but I gave no response to his question, not really believing that he was aware of me. Time passed and he resumed his position in front of the computer, looking at his notes although I could now feel a slight tension in his thoughts.

Conscious now of my movements and frightened of his reaction, I watched him carefully from afar trying to work out his thoughts, yet he was difficult to read; it was as if he'd put up a constant wall that was impossible to break through.

After a while I gained the confidence to move a little closer, to study his face as he continued with his work. It showed no recognition of me, no sign of fear; of course I was cloaked and he would be unable to see me even if I was not, surely?

Sitting down at the desk I noted the time on the wall; now 01:17am. I looked back at Leon who seemed to think time was insignificant. He looked around the room sharply, as if trying to locate something he needed before standing and leaving, seemingly headed for another room, unafraid of the dark.

I stayed at the desk and decided to move his notebook a little to the left, a small but playful experiment of mine. Next, I put my finger in the glass of water that lay in front of it before letting two drops spill onto the desk.

Nervously, I waited for his return looking towards the dark space of the door. Soon enough, Leon entered the room looking the same as when he'd left. He was carrying a book, large and leather-bound it was covered in dust. It's title was faded, but apart from being large it was a very plain-looking example.

I watched as he sat down in front of me, glancing briefly at the changes on his desk before picking up the notebook and flicking through to his old notes. I'd seen his expression change, if only slightly but he had noticed what I had done.

So why was he trying to hide it? Unsure of what to do next, I contemplated the last encounter with David while I watched Leon work silently. The only sound was the typing of the keys on his laptop and it made me feel close to him. I wanted to touch the keys and remembered the way I used to write with my own laptop, the stories I used to write about fashion, politics, you name it.

I began to grow more distressed as I ran thoughts through my head, and slowly I stood up and moved towards the end of the room. I was completely alone and suddenly the idea that I could never really know Leon Cardew really hit home.

Even though I'd been dead for what must have been a few months, my feelings never ceased to surprise me. It was as if I was going through the mourning process but for myself, each new revelation of the things I'd lost hitting me just as hard as the last.

Perhaps the soul never gets used to death, although more recently things have got easier for me. However seeing Leon that night really reminded me how much I would miss sharing intimacies with another soul.

The feelings I'd experienced at the desk were familiar to ones I'd known in my life; nervousness, desire, happiness. Yet why would I feel this way towards him now that I was dead, I told myself it really was ridiculous.

I felt a deep feeling, like a wave sweep through me and suddenly I realised all was not right in the room. Turning around I saw Leon was staring right at the spot where I stood, although irrationally I knew that he was staring right at me.

I froze, completely silent as I watched his expression; it was deadly serious and difficult to read. He had turned in his chair, just staring and I realised I'd let my guard down, that perhaps I hadn't been cloaked as well as I'd thought. Even still, most ordinary humans cannot see spirits, at least in the conventional way; most of them never even try.

Suddenly he spoke right at me, his voice once again breaking the sweet silence.

"Who are you? Why are you here?" He asked the question into what could have been thin air but he asked it, almost as if he could sense me, as if he knew I was there. I couldn't speak, suddenly terrified and confused by the direct way he'd questioned me; it was most unexpected.

If Mr Cardew had been aware of my activities he had been a bloody good actor not to have shown the slightest sign of detection.

"I know you're there, I've been aware of you ever since you entered," Leon spoke again, his voice deep but pleasant, his words shocking to me, "Why did you move my things? You thought I wouldn't notice, or is it a game?"

"I…" Shaking I couldn't quite find the words to talk, instead deciding to leave the library in my own personal turmoil. It swept through the room, unable to take my eyes off of him; Leon Cardew, beautiful librarian.

He sensed what I was about to do and moving awkwardly, just before my exit I heard him shout, "No, please! Don't leave!"

I left him there, in darkness to wonder what demon had been with him that night.

Chapter Sixteen

I began to watch him from a distance, utterly captivated but unsure of how to proceed forward, if at all. I still don't understand why I returned to the library, but something drew me towards it – towards him - like a beacon. Perhaps it was just Leon and his unusual beauty, his energy that attracted me for reasons I did not know.

Perhaps he had the key that I was searching for, a way through to help Alex or to find the way for myself; forgive the eager ambitions but it was as if we were meant to meet that night.

But because he was already aware of me, I knew it was dangerous. It took courage for me to approach him again, and for the past two nights I had been unable to summon that courage, fearing him like a child that shied away from strangers.

My heart was in no way closed to this new person and the part of myself I kept deep within, safe and blanketed was wary of him. But still, nothing had changed; no solution had appeared in front of me like the light that I hoped would someday illuminate to take me away from this world.

It once occurred to me that it would not be light but instead it would be darkness, reflecting on the monster I had become. That thought frightened me and my loneliness echoed even sharper in my mind, forcing me closer to Leon as if he could solve everything I had to throw at him.

I half expected the old building to be empty when I got there, as most other libraries surely were at 11pm. But even before I entered, I sensed him inside the same small, dimly-lit room; the exact spot where I'd left him two nights before.

The knowledge did something to my 'heart' or maybe just my soul. I felt excited, yet strangely vulnerable as if this man could destroy me in ways that Gabrielle could never manage;

silly of me to consider him a threat yet a delicious one at that. It was then I realised I wanted something from him, but the reason cloaked itself – what could I possibly want other than Alex's safety?

At first I kept my distance, afraid of scaring him away from his work and also a bit fearful of what he'd do if he realised it was me. It was curious; watching his reactions they didn't seem appropriately shocked, a normal reaction of those that come into contact with the dead.

As I watched him work from the doorway, he gave no sign that he was aware of my presence in the room. I began to wonder if he knew the extent of his gift to detect spirits. He didn't seem to be a novice, but there seemed to be innocence about him, his life, and his fragility that made him beautiful to me.

Apart from the two of us, the building was empty of souls both dead and alive so I reasoned with myself that he was hardly a magnet. Only to me.

How can you see me, I thought to myself as I watched him continue with his menial work, typing away with a swiftness and vigour that I once associated with myself.

Not once did his typing falter as I almost subconsciously moved forward; drawn to him yet afraid of him.

I continued to watch Leon, slowly growing closer to him as the nights moved on yet he gave no sign that he knew. In an odd way, I grew almost attached to this strange man yet I couldn't possibly know him – not from life and certainly never from death.

As I observed his behaviour and became accustomed to his routine, the invisible barrier between us seemed to become thinner, almost as if it were not really there.

Eventually I found the confidence to approach him, my intentions now blurred in my mind. I can't even remember now what I wanted of this creature, Leon Cardew but my need would not leave me until it had been settled.

I found myself in the small room where he worked once more, but this time I did not try to conceal myself from his human eyes. As I entered swiftly, I let the papers blow off the desks around me and immediately he stopped typing.

Slowly I watched as he turned towards me, his eyes searching for some sign of an intruder; I don't know what he saw but his eyes seemed to settle on me.

"Is...is anyone there?" He asked, hesitantly, a mild hint of fear in his bright blue eyes. He was dressed in black; a shade he often wore as he worked. It was a cold night and he was wearing a turtleneck sweater and black jeans, the same leather jacket slung over his chair – black, of course.

Once again his striking features hit me; for once it was as if he was staring straight at me, unwavering and sure of my presence in the room.

"Yes, I'm here," I spoke to him for the very first time, and visibly he recoiled at the sound of my voice, I continued, "but I can leave if you want me to."

His pale skin seemed to turn even paler, and shaking his head he stayed silent for mere seconds before saying, "No, don't do that...were you here before?"

"Yes. I must confess I've been watching you, I'm sorry if that scares you," I replied.

He sighed, as if he knew deep down that it was the truth – we both knew it, although he had a slight disadvantage over me and I could tell, even though he was trying to be strong about it, that he was scared.

His hand was shaky as he reached for his glass of water; the same glass that I'd moved on that fateful first night. Every night he would rinse out the glass, wash it and leave it on the draining board of the small bright kitchen, ready and waiting like a faithful servant. His routines amused me, and I smiled.

"Why are you here, who are you?" He asked after he sipped from the glass, still facing the direction of my voice. I moved closer, but stopped when I saw him visibly recoil, although he tried to hold it back.

"My name's not important...when I saw you something in me changed, Leon. It was an accident - my being here, believe me on that," I tried to speak softly, reassuringly yet I could tell he was inwardly terrified of my presence in the library.

"You know I've…sensed things before, long before this but I've never…let them know I was aware. But you're different, I've never felt it so strong before," he told me, seeming to calm slightly with the reinforcement of words. They seemed to fall from his lips with an ease of poetry, giving the impression that their meaning was sharpened by his voice. It transfixed me.

I moved around the room, his gaze somehow able to follow me although I knew by now that he couldn't actually see me – his senses were in-tune with me nevertheless.

After a few moments of silence he asked, "Are you still there? I can feel you're there."

"I know. I couldn't help but feel drawn to you, but now I'm here I feel utterly lost," I whispered, unable to conjure up any more meaning than before, "I feel stuck in this world and now someone I used to be close to is in danger."

"So you think I'll be able to help you?" He seemed to consider the idea with an air of bemusement and seriousness that I couldn't quite work out.

"I don't know anymore…I was murdered, that's all I know."

He started out of his chair, but his hand slipped and suddenly he looked very weak and shaken. I moved towards him unable to stop myself, I reached out to him but he recoiled from me again.

Quickly he got up, and said, "I'm sorry, I can't do this right now."

To my surprise, he walked swiftly across the room and grabbed his coat as I stood beside the computer, not daring to approach him.

Then he was gone, into the night as if nothing had happened. The only remainder of the incident lay still lit up on his desk; the laptop. Beside it, the glass of water still half full, the notebook lying open beside it.

The presence of his belongings was of small comfort to me, but I hoped he would return to them and with a stupid hope, to me.

Well, what could I do? I waited for him to come back, but that night was a lonely one for me. When the laptop eventually ran out of power, the darkness filled the room and the library was still.

For a while I was afraid that I would miss his return, that he would choose somewhere else to do his work and that the next day he would collect his laptop and leave this place and his job.

Nevertheless when I returned to the library the next night, I did not have to wait long before he entered the building. There he was, his black leather jacket slung over his arm; the familiar sight of Leon relieving me in a way I thought I'd lost, buried somewhere in the past remains of my life.

He looked tense at first, unsure of whether he was alone but I waited in the same room, 'his' room, where hopefully he'd expect me.

I was sat in his chair when he arrived, and at once he seemed to look at me in the way that I remembered, his bright blue eyes almost piercing me with their sharpness.

"I thought you might be here," he said, almost nonplussed at my presence.

Casually he hung his jacket over a nearby chair and then pulled it over to the desk, an attempt perhaps not to disturb me.

"Why did you leave like that?" I asked him, "I missed you."

He laughed out loud, almost sarcastically at this last comment, before telling me, "It's complicated, I'm sure if you wanted to you could have followed me to find out."

"I respect you too much for that," I replied, softly and sincerely, "besides, I knew you'd come back to me."

He looked surprised at that, "You mean that, don't you?"

I nodded, and he seemed to register my agreement which puzzled me. He looked up at me, and his words surprised me.

"Do you want to know how I can do that? To be honest, I have no fucking idea but why don't I go and get a coffee and then I'll explain it to you the best I can."

I sat frozen in the chair while he got up and wandered towards a small kitchen on the other side of the building. It was almost like he had changed dramatically overnight; he was chatty, relaxed in his own atmosphere and prepared to talk to the ghost that had terrified him the night before.

I was still pondering over his personality change when he returned with a mug of coffee in his hand.

"I would offer you one, but you know…" he said, humour in his voice, "Before we go any further, I want to know your name. After all, you know mine."

"Do you think you can handle it?" I asked, his reply consisting of an ironic look.

"Okay," I said, "My name is Night Swallow. That's my real name, I was a travel journalist murdered here in London."

He seemed to think about the information before accepting it, no recognition registering on his face.

"Nope, never heard of you," he told me, "but then I'm just a librarian."

"You're a very good librarian," I replied, amused at the repertoire we'd already built up, "so, why don't you tell me about your abilities?"

He took a considered sip of his coffee and waited an almost agonising period of time before speaking.

"Well," he started, "It's never been something I embraced, even as a child. The first time it happened, it scared me shitless.

"Tell me about it," I said, intrigued. He paused, about to speak before seemingly changing his mind before he opened his mouth.

"Wait, you've been watching me since the first time I confronted you? Why did it take you so long to speak…don't tell me you're shy?"

Now it was my turn to laugh. I took a deep breath and said, "Well actually I was amazed by your ability and yes, you scared me. I didn't know how you'd react."

He sighed, nodding shortly and tapping his fingers on the chair, before leaning closer and beginning his tale.

"Okay, when it first happened I was nine years old. One Saturday morning I awoke to see a strange Indian figure, like a goddess standing at the end of my bed. She was some sort of ancient spirit, dressed in full ritual dress and I was just paralysed there watching her.

"Eventually she turned around and walked right through the wall."

I listened as he explained a series of childhood visitations and 'moments' when things weren't always quite right, and he told me how he'd got used to blocking out the visions and ignoring anything that approached him, mostly out of fear.

"God this feels weird, talking out loud like this to an empty room," he said with a touch of humour in his smile.

"Pity you can't see me, it might have made you more at ease," I replied, failing to mention that talking to him also felt odd.

"I never asked for this 'gift', I didn't want it. When I was about seventeen, I hadn't seen a ghost for around a year and I thought I'd got rid of them for good. I was hanging out with my friends and by that time I had a girlfriend, called Claire."

"Some nights I'd stay over at her place, but we'd have to stay really quiet because her parents would never have allowed it if they knew. Anyway I decided to go home that night, through the window, you know, said goodnight and that I'd see her the next day."

"The next part is what she told me. She was starting to fall asleep when she heard the window open a crack and when she turned she saw me climb inside and get in bed next to her. She said she put her arms around me because I was cold, but I didn't say a word and later I turned over and rolled out of bed.

"She thought I'd fallen out, that it was pretty funny but when she leaned over there was no-one there. Then she realised she never actually heard the drop...that's when she screamed."

I shifted in the chair, intrigued by the story, "So if that wasn't you, then...?"

He shrugged, unsure of what to say as he took another sip of the coffee and leaned back against the wall.

"Maybe it was something...pretending to be me, to get my attention. Or maybe it was me, somehow," he continued, looking thoughtful, "I do have a theory though."

"What's that?" I asked, completely hooked.

"Well, there was…this thing that I used to see quite often, say out the corner of my eye, or in the mirror when I was shaving. Just for a split second I'd see him, and then he was gone. I always got the same feeling when I saw him, of idleness and hatred."

"Did you ever find out who he was?" I asked.

"That's the interesting part. Every time I caught sight of him, I saw a likeness of myself but I could never catch him long enough to be sure. When I was twenty my mother told me that she'd had a miscarriage while carrying me in the womb. She didn't realise she was still pregnant until she got bigger and doctors told her she had conceived twins."

"So you think it was your twin?" I asked, a feeling of slight uneasiness coming over me.

"I don't know," he replied, also slightly unsure of how to explain it, "but if you see any other spirits around that look like me, then I'd appreciate you letting me know. Wait, are we alone right now?"

"Yes," I answered with complete honesty, "There are no other spirits in the building, which I found strange since you seemed to draw me in like a magnet."

"I've always been like that with the ladies…" he said, jokingly.

My silence said it all.

It was difficult to imagine the sort of bond that I began to feel with Leon; it was unnatural, some might say wrong and most definitely weird – more to Leon than to me.

But something about it also felt right…it stopped me feeling so alone in myself. Yet part of me expected Gabrielle to intervene the way she had at the medium's house.

However I have to stress that I did not feel unsettled in Leon's company, quite the opposite in fact and as we gradually moved on to the subject of my situation, I began to open up to this mortal man who listened to my every word with a rapture I could never had conceived of before now.

I told him of my travels and of my past relationship with Alex, the beach nightmare and most of all, Amon.

"He killed those people like they were nothing to him," I repeated the story that had haunted me ever since with all the sincerity and simplicity I could manage; "I hid like a coward while this happened. And then I saw him somehow...change. They were sitting by the fire and he was chanting, the police were coming up right behind them and he was chanting like someone possessed."

At first he didn't understand what I meant, how someone could switch bodies the way I described but then it became clearer and with visible horror he told me something new.

"There was once a legend of a curse," he told me, quietly and with hesitance, "I suppose the location would be about right actually. It was about an ancient curse or spell, given to the 'master' as it were, and embodied in an object that had considerable meaning to them. Each time the master wanted to retrieve the ritual it would be performed on the desired new host and the master would be able to body swap."

"Body swap? I didn't think that was humanly possible," I replied.

"Well, I doubt he is what we'd consider 'human' anymore. You see, when the bond is created, a demon is supposedly summoned into a particular object, and part of the host's soul - in this case Amon's - would also be placed into the object.

"He own soul would become distorted and demon-like in itself, until eventually it would distort his whole being."

"What is it, voodoo?" I asked, unbelieving that he could have heard of such a thing.

"Something like that, it's probably much darker and almsot forgotten in eastern countries. It's a very old tale though, I wonder just how old this Amon is and what he's capable of."

I smiled softly, "You're very accepting, you know. You trust me."

He laughed at this, unsure of what to say and as he pondered on it I fixed my energies on the room, listening intently for signs of another soul. There was still nothing, we were safe.

"I know you're who you say you are...I can just feel you," he hesitated, before saying, "Look, I don't know how the hell this happened but maybe this is something I need, too."

I looked into his eyes, bright blue and unwavering, as I tried to work out the meaning in his last words. It was funny, how he still remained closed to me almost as if he'd put a wall up around his innermost thoughts and feelings.

"What if he finds Alex?" I asked now, my mood darkening in thoughts, "what happens then? I can't bear to think about it."

Leon seemed to be staring into a spot in the distance, contemplating the situation with a seriousness that merited my attention, yet I had nothing left to say. The silence was a small comfort to me, our strange unity seeming to make sense in the small hours of the morning.

Within the next few nights it turned out we had plenty to say to each other. We talked about modern politics, news and the things that I had missed in my death. Although I wasn't as up-to-date as he was, I still managed to make him laugh in our strange dance of words.

We talked about our childhoods, past relationships and most of all, Mr Cardew and his abilities.

Although we got on well together in the strangest possible circumstances, he wasn't loud or confident at all. He was actually rather quiet and when he did talk about himself it was always with a very mild tone of voice and a wry smile. I noticed that when he was talking, I found it sweeter than I'd ever thought possible while watching him from the shadows, and I wondered what secrets he still kept from me, a spirit who hung on his every word.

I eventually realised I wanted to take care of him, to protect him for his fragility and humanness struck me as something I could never touch or hold, and it scared me how easily it could be lost.

It was the fact that he was alive, his heart, the blood pumping around his body and the softness of his skin; all of those things made him almost like something sacred and I felt a guilt at even daring to speak to this creature. It began to sadden me that we could never be more than what we were, but what we had achieved together was nothing short of a miracle in itself.

About a week after we spoke properly, Leon decided to look up my story on the internet. I'd told him it'd been quite a big media story at the time, the journalist who's witnessed a massacre in Thailand and lived to tell the tale.

I joked that they would have been happier if I'd managed to take pictures too, but he was quite serious about finding me and didn't respond. It didn't take long to search for my name and then there it was; my picture.

He was silent for a while as the story loaded up on the screen, and I wondered again what he was thinking. It was an okay picture, I was standing on the beach in Satun looking slightly worn, my hair was a mess but I was happy to be alive.

It felt like such a long time ago, and seeing myself like that really brought home the fact that I was now so alone and stuck in this world. I felt like crying, if only it were so easy to cry. My heart bled pain but what was the use of such intense emotions without a body to express them in?

I looked at him as he stared at the screen.

"So, that's you," he said.

"Yes, not the best picture in the world," I said, trying to sound upbeat.

"I don't know what I expected…you look so real and well, pretty beautiful."

He was staring at my picture and I began to feel hurt building up inside, making me want to scream at the injustice of it all. It wasn't Leon's fault, but I could tell he sensed the shift in moods.

I sighed, excused myself and left the library that night to gather my thoughts, delving deeper into my psyche than I had in a long time. It was the picture, why did I have to look at the picture…I was hurt, but I swore I would return to Leon.

I went back to Magnus's room, the place which now felt, rightly or wrongly, like somewhere I belonged. After a while, when the night was coming to a close I felt something stir in the air around me and I sensed the vague smell of perfume.

Looking around the room I saw nothing, but an overpowering sense of unease told me otherwise. The mirror beckoned me and as I looked into its dusty darkness, old and marked with time, there came a face; it was Gabrielle.

All fear left my soul as I stared at her there, her face calm but serious and her eyes barely visible enough to show her anger – or how I imagined it. Her rage echoed inside me and the image of her was enough to shake me. I held still to the spot, and waited for what she had to say.

Her lips moved in slow deliberately formed words and I could just about see the purple in her eyes as she spoke to me in words that chilled. There was coldness in her voice, yet it was so obvious a part of her, almost like an internal voice that belonged to something deeper within her.

"Do you wish to cause this man harm?" The familiar voice asked, "Leave him alone, he is no good for you and you are no good to him."

It was a warning, and as she moved back into the shadows I turned sharply to see absolutely nothing, the scent gone like a figment of my imagination – a fragment of Gabrielle that would haunt me just as much as the lights that never came.

I stayed there staring into the mirror for quite a while, emotionless and stripped like I was nothing at all. The mirror reflected nothing, as I knew it would and I willed it to show my face.

For mere moments I imagined I saw the outline of my face, and forcing out my energy I tried to make it become more real. A crack started to appear down the mirror as I forced it even further and for a moment, there I was.

My unruly hair took up most of the mirror, yet it blurred around the edges like it was not entirely there. My eyes shone almost gold in the light, and I felt the energy inside me almost catch on fire with the effort of it all.

I looked real yet my face was twisted with torment at the concentration it took and the force on the mirror. Suddenly the cracks exploded all over the mirror and with finality I vanished from the shards.

I felt like I was going insane, spiralling down into the depths of my own soul - is that is what I can call it - until light came to catch up with me as it always did.

Chapter Seventeen

The next night I 'awoke' in the way that my kind do, to something very extraordinary. It was Gabrielle, I could sense her calling to me from somewhere in London but it was calling in the most obscure sense.

In a confused state I looked around the room to find that nothing had been disturbed; my old master's possessions lay in the dusty, messy collection that had been practically untouched since his departure.

It was times like these I wished he was still around to guide me, if only he'd told me of Gabrielle and what she was capable of. I felt like a cornered rabbit, unable to escape her grasp – yet I knew I had to answer her.

At first I failed to understand why she would reveal herself to me, for she was always invisible, undetectable. I knew that it was deliberate, but to follow her brought up cold shivers in the very essence of my soul. Something felt very wrong.

When my mind starting to clear and confidence answered my fears, I left the comfort of the room and, with hesitance I followed my instinct to somewhere that made no real sense to me.

It was a council estate in one of the rougher parts of London, and at first it appeared deserted of all life. The walls were covered heavily with graffiti and windows were boarded up in the tower blocks around me.

The wind howled through the streets and I did not feel safe as I waited for a sign or sound. I listened very carefully to the small voices on the ground, but they were just ordinary people and gave nothing away.

I could feel something; her presence, but Gabrielle failed to appear. I wished she would just tell me what was going on so for a few moments I decided to wait. Later, I regretted my decision.

A gang of youths had appeared from one of the doorways around the corner and had started to walk south towards my direction. They were talking and spitting and carrying bottles of alcohol in brown crumpled bags.

They were all male and wore dark hoods which were concealing most of their faces, some of them kicking objects on the ground and generally looking riled. The air held a sense of anger and I felt reproachful of them.

One of them wore a baseball cap, and walked with a swagger that made him look like he'd recently undergone a hip replacement. The scene reminded me of the supposed London's gang culture, an investigative journalist's dream.

I began to feel very wary of the situation when I spotted their apparent destination; they were headed towards a larger gang who were gathered outside a bus stop. It was dark and the surrounding lights had been broken, making them difficult to see at first glance.

I couldn't believe she had led me to this scene, couldn't understand her reason for having an interest in this pathetic-looking place. It was almost depressing, the way people had to live in estates like this one.

Still Gabrielle did not show and as the gang moved closer to the bus stop I watched in growing dread as one of them finished their bottle and smashed it against a nearby wall, attracting the attention of the neighbouring gang.

I kept my distance, watching from one of the tower buildings as they began to shout obscenities to each other. The youth in the cap looked about eighteen, with pale skin and freckles. I watched as he provoked one of the girls from the bus stop, before pushing her to the ground before running back and shouting more abuse.

"You're a fucking slag!" he shouted, his body tense and ready for a fight.

One of the boys smashed his bottle against the wall of the bus stop, alcohol pouring out he began to walk sharply towards the other gang. I saw that he was black, and he was quickly followed by two larger males also wearing hoods.

I heard one of the approaching gang shout, "What the fuck do you think you're doing over here man, that's just disrespect right there! Get out of here now or I'll fucking do you!"

There came a response from the other side and both gangs stopped in their tracks, considering each other. The atmosphere was thick with anger and I knew that before long, I would witness a violent attack.

I felt unable to move, helpless to stop the situation and memories came flooding back of the beach. The bodies, the drug baron…Amon. I had been powerless then, quelled by my fear to stop them from their massacre. I was powerless now, but in an entirely different way.

The guy from the bus stop seemed cool, calm and collected before saying, "I ain't scared of you, so you better back off."

They started to taunt him, showing they weren't afraid and I watched him stand his ground, looking strong as a horse, tall and hard to read. His expression was concealed half under his hood and half in the darkness.

The worst part was, I could feel their emotions; they were full of hatred and bravado, anger and invincibility. It was a terrible mixture and it disturbed me so much that I wanted to leave, screw Gabrielle.

Seeming to sense my thoughts Gabrielle appeared beside me, as if watching a movie play out she looked fascinated by it all.

"Look at them, true warriors are they not? That one there is Jake, he's very strong." She said, her voice icy and full of admiration for the determined gang – especially the black boy who was standing his ground.

I looked at her in surprise, "How can you say that? Why did you bring me here, I don't want to see this."

She laughed, finding my remarks humorous, "Because you need to understand that death is integral to life and also, not to interfere with it."

Jake was shouting at the gang, his face twisting into insults as he pushed closer into the rival gang. One of them was holding the sharp broken neck of the bottle, shaking it and warning him off but Jake was in the zone.

"You do know they're going to kill him for that, don't you?" I asked, shocked at her attitude and her apparent enjoyment at this pre-massacre.

"Of course I know, innocent girl," Gabrielle responded, "That's why I am here."

I started to back away from her, cold and filled with horror at her words but then my attention focused on the threatening gang as the ringleader pulled out a knife and stuck it into Jake's chest.

"Shit! Gabrielle, do something!" I cried, as she looked on with a quiet smile.

"I will, when he's dead," she replied, seemingly happy with the turn of events.

The gang scattered as the ringleader pulled out his knife and stabbed Jake again and again while at the other side, one of the bus-stop gang threw a bottle and shouted in anger for him to stop.

Jake stayed silent, kneeling on the ground clasping his bleeding torso as the last of the rival gang ran into the shadows. Then Jake collapsed.

Gabrielle spoke beside me, her eyes unmoving from the scene, "This is what it's come down to, Night. The world is full of pain, of death and suffering. Eventually it all comes to an end – it has to. These scenes fill the living world every day, they respect nothing and they die for nothing. This is something you need to accept."

It was a difficult thing to watch, the death of another person but I found myself unable to move as I witnessed the same thing that had once happened to me.

I saw his ghost separate from his body and as he dazedly looked around, I saw Gabrielle shift and slowly move down towards the confused spirit.

I hastily followed her, keeping my distance as I watched her approach him. He was silent as he turned to see his dead body, crumpled on the wet dirty ground in a puddle of blood.

He turned sharply as Gabrielle said, "Do not be afraid, child."

"Who-who are you? What happened? I'm dead, right?" He asked, panicky and scared. Gabrielle nodded, an evil smile spread on her face.

"Stay close to me, whatever you do. Watch very carefully." She said as I began to feel a terrible mass of darkness approach us from the shadows; it almost hurt, and I felt like I was being sucked into it before I even saw what it was.

It came from below, a large black moving cloud, shapeless and frantic it had come for Jake. I didn't know how I knew but I dreaded this thing nevertheless as it moved towards the newly-formed spirit.

He stared at it in dumb shock and awe, unable to run he looked to Gabrielle for help like a pathetic puppy and not like the brave 'warrior' he had shown himself to be in front of the 'hoodies' that plagued the council estate like hyenas picking off the weak.

Gabrielle nodded in amusement and she stepped in-between the force of darkness and the cowering Jake. Suddenly a huge flash of golden light emanated from her and I felt its power almost paralyse me in fear.

Gabrielle was pushing the force back from Jake, and also from me and all I could do was look on in shock as it moved away, seeming to melt in her light. Soon it was gone and all that was left was a lingering feeling deep inside me, like it had taken away some of my happiness.

I knew somehow that it couldn't really affect me, shouldn't affect me, that the dark mass had been intended for Jake and no-one else.

As I stared at Gabrielle I worked out what she had done; she'd saved Jake, stopped him from going where he was supposed to in favour of what? Being her servant, joining her motley crew of spirits, for what?

Somehow she knew what would happen tonight, pre-planned this little addition to her group – perhaps she'd even been eying up this particular 'chav' for a long time.

Jake looked terrified, unable to take his eyes off the spot where the dark thing had first appeared as if it would return. Eventually he turned to Gabrielle.

"Who are you? And what was that?!" He asked, sounding confused and a shadow of what I saw just a few moments from his death.

Gabrielle responded, "I am Gabrielle, and you're mine now, Jake." She said his name with almost disgust, as she walked forwards through the council estate. He followed her, eagerly but anxiously. I looked on in pity.

"And Night," the voice echoed through the estate, "You don't have to get involved in this, but it might benefit you to join me. I don't admit to understanding you, but Magnus trusted you, therefore you have my respects. Meet me at the hotel tomorrow at 12am, I have some information you might be interested to hear..."

Before they disappeared around the corner, Jake turned to look at me just once and I knew right there and then, that I would probably never see him again. I hoped they would swallow him up into their little collective – her collective – and that I'd never come face-to-face with his kind again.

Chapter Eighteen

Leon sat in his chair, eyebrows raised as he listened to my tales of woe from Malaysia. I told him about the time I'd lost my light-travel bag, containing most of my fresh clothes and travellers cheques in the middle of a terrible downpour of rain.

He looked comfortable, warm and relaxed as we spoke in the way we'd both become accustomed to, he even laughed occasionally. I felt it was a worthy distraction after the things I'd witnessed the night before.

"So, you were basically fucked then?" He asked in good humour.

I nodded, "It was awful, and to make it worse, some local guy with a fondness for white chicks thought I was a prostitute and asked me how much!"

He smiled, before replying, "Well, from your picture, you can't blame a guy for trying."

"Har har," I replied sarcastically.

Folding his legs under him, he confessed, "I wish I was able to travel more, that is something I regret."

"Well, you may not be a spring chicken but I'm sure you could still manage it. Drop the security, the job, the stable living and just go for it."

He stayed silent, before shaking his head sadly, "Nah, not anymore…I had my chance."

I knew there were words between us left unsaid, but I was pre-occupied by Gabrielle's offer and the odd meeting she had mentioned before leaving me alone once again to face my demons.

Still, I had many questions that needed answered, like the dark mass that almost swamped me in its unstoppable force. I could still feel its aftermath deep inside me.

I wanted to know what she did to banish it, how the light seemed to emanate from her like something God-given. I was also sure that God had nothing to do with it, but her power both intrigued me and terrified me at the same time.

She was building an army, but what was the purpose of it all? I failed to understand why she kept Jake for her own, like a possession for her to master.

There was a darkness rooted deep inside her, swallowing up lost souls and those with dangerous ruthlessness. It made me ponder what kind of future I had to look forward to while I stayed in this world.

Leon seemed to sense my unease, and asked, "Ms Swallow, what's wrong? You seem different tonight."

I sighed, "This whole being dead thing seems to hold a bigger responsibility than I first thought. Although I'm not yet sure what that responsibility is."

He looked confused. I wanted to tell him what had happened the night before, about Gabrielle and the spirits she was guiding in the wrong direction – her direction. It would have taken off so much pressure, to unload my worries onto him but I couldn't bring myself to do it.

I realised I wanted to protect him, to shield him from harm and the fact that I was already talking to him may put him in danger. He shifted in his chair, looking uncomfortable.

I looked at his watch; it was approaching 12 so either way I had to leave and I accepted this with quick regret.

"I'm sorry, I have to go." I said.

"Washing your hair?" He replied, seeming to acknowledge my change of personality.

"A meeting," I responded cryptically, before briskly forcing myself to leave his company.

The hotel looked unwelcoming as I approached with thoughts of Leon in my mind. I forced them out, aware not to leave traces of him for Gabrielle to mock. Chances were, she knew I'd visited him but I really felt like challenging her and her gang of misfit ghosts to punish me.

As I entered the room I saw that Jake was sitting on the bed, facing the window were snow had started to fall outside.

"Jake?" I said, a little surprised to find him in her room and slightly angry that she had instructed him to wait for me.

"She'll be with you soon," he replied, before turning to me with an earnest look on his face I did not recognise from the young thug I'd seen the night before.

"Look, she's really done a lot for me. Listen to what I have to say…Gabrielle is-."

"No, please, I don't want to get involved in this," I responded firmly, interrupting his speech. His tone surprised me, it wasn't at all what I expected and his presence alone was making me feel paranoid.

"You disgust me," I told him, "Get out and tell Gabrielle I don't have the patience for this."

He nodded, stood up and looked back at me as he left the room; the look in his eyes caught me off guard and made me wonder exactly what Gabrielle had done to him.

As I looked around the room I realised that nothing had changed since my last visit, apart from one thing; a framed black and white photograph of Gabrielle from her stage days. It appeared to be signed in thick black ink, as was the style in those days.

"Do I look the same?" A voice from behind startled me, although I was able to keep myself from looking at her.

Instead, I nodded and replied, "Apart from the look on your face – so innocent."

Gabrielle smiled behind me, and slowly I turned around to see her looking dark, sophisticated and strangely beautiful. No lipstick smudged her face and there was no blood on her hands – she looked clean.

"What do you want from me Gabrielle?" I asked, my tone demanding with no sign of unease – not quite what I felt inside.

"I have something which might be of interest to you," she told me, a knowing look in her eyes that worried me greatly. I look at her with suspicion.

"And why would you care about that?" I asked.

"Because there might be something we can do for each other," she replied, her voice smooth like velvet.

"What could you possibly do for me, without you taking my soul?" I told her, amused.

"Look," I continued, "I'm not interested in your offer whatever it might be."

Angry, I prepared to leave the hotel room when her words stopped me in my tracks.

"Let's just say I've been keeping tabs on an old friend of yours…"

With that she disappeared as quickly as a dart of light through the open window, and I shielded myself from her in fear. When I realised it was safe, I looked out the window after her, feeling the powerful wind run through me.

Infuriated but curious of her last comment, I decided I had no option but to follow her in the way that she had so obviously planned.

This time it wasn't difficult to track her; she'd made it perfectly clear she wanted me to accompany her but annoyingly, the location was something she kept to herself.

Part of me hoped it didn't involve another death viewing, but after her comment the other conclusion seemed far worse.

It was difficult to concentrate as the wind blew against me, but I knew I was close to her, almost under her protection as we neared our destination.

Finally she stopped and when I caught up with her, we were outside a night club called Opulence. It was the back entrance and we appeared to be alone.

"Why have you brought me here?" I demanded, once again trying to reinstate my power to no avail.

"Be patient, you'll see," Gabrielle replied.

It wasn't long before we were joined in the back courtyard by a man wearing a dark suit, and carrying a plain black briefcase. He looked around suspiciously before waiting in the corner. At first I thought he was nothing special.

"Recognise him?" Gabrielle asked, as if trying to provoke a response.

I looked at her, confused at the question but when she did not react, I moved down towards the man. His skin was a light olive, and I could smell a strong perfume that was vaguely familiar.

And then it clicked. I realised the man I was standing just inches from was Amon the murderer and Amon the body-snatcher. I recoiled with fright, temporarily forgetting the guard I'd put up from Gabrielle and even the fact that he could not hurt me.

Shaking, I looked at him in disgust, unable to summon words as my emotions spiralled out of control in a litany of anger, confusion, fear and loathing.

"Come back, before you do something you'll regret," I heard Gabrielle call me. I didn't respond, really couldn't care less what she wanted me to do.

She must have sensed my emotions because seconds later, I was pulled back with a violent force.

"You have to listen to me, Night," she told me, "This is not up to you right now!"

"How could you know about this and not tell me?!" I cried, directing my anger towards Gabrielle instead.

"Be still, you must not let your feelings interfere at this delicate situation," she replied, her calmness seeming to influence me enough that I no longer felt like charging at my killer.

"This person is a monster," I stated, the hatred and revulsion showing in my voice, "he does not deserve to live."

"My point exactly," replied Gabrielle, my shock and horror forcing me to take my eyes off Amon and to look into hers. They were cold, staring and coldly serious.

"What do you mean by that? What are you planning to do?" I asked her in amazement as I tried to control my voice. It was hard, seeing him like that.

My questions were met by the slightest of smiles, almost undetectable to anyone but me.

"Your little friend Alex has been getting ahead of himself, as I'm sure you already know," she told me, sending what felt like pins into my heart.

"What do you know of him, leave him alone!" I cried, unable to stop myself.

"Shhh," Gabrielle replied, mockingly, "He's getting closer to the prize. Now, I take it you want to save your stupid ex from certain death, don't you?"

I nodded; fear seizing me almost completely at the thought of Alex in trouble and at that moment I hated myself for not being able to do something about it. I looked into her eyes searchingly, looking for an answer and finding cold steel in its place.

"Alex has gained knowledge of Amon's whereabouts, through sources here in London," she told me as I listened in surprise, "He's going to follow him to a meeting point, the fool. Chances are that he'll get caught; he's reckless, hungry for some justice over your death. Pity he doesn't know that the charm he's wearing around his neck will lead to the looming finality of his death."

"J-just tell me what you want," I said, my emotions showing her exactly how weak I really was. I couldn't help it, couldn't store my feelings the way she did. I felt disarmed, shocked and also angry with myself that I hadn't known how close Alex was to finding my killer.

"This is the all-powerful 'monster' known to some as Amon. He's an old soul, older than you'll ever know – pure evil. And you're right; he shouldn't be alive, allowed to roam the streets searching for his next victim. But you took something very important to him, Night, you naughty girl," Gabrielle continued, "And now he's frantically searching for it in places he shouldn't; just asking for trouble. He could be getting desperate, plus his body is weakening – he's using again, that's why switching bodies so often is necessary. That first high must really be something special."

As if in answer to her words, Amon was joined by a younger male from the back door of the club. Dressed in a dark tracksuit and wearing a gold necklace around his neck, I watched him approach with his hands in his pockets.

"What does this have to do with you, what's the connection here?" I asked, growing impatient at her story. I glanced back to the courtyard in time to see the swap taking place. Gabrielle was right, it was drugs. Amon pocketed the package quickly and I heard him mumble something to the younger guy.

Looking impartial, Gabrielle said, "You want to save your friend Alex, don't you? We both want Amon dead, so I'd be willing to overlook your intervention with the living for his…departure from his current body. Can you imagine the power in a spirit so old?"

Shocked at her proposal, I replied, "That's ridiculous! Gabrielle you can't possibly be serious, you can't control him. You said it yourself, he's a monster!"

She laughed, taking in my fear without giving away a single thing. I looked at her defiantly, unable to believe what she'd just told me.

"I have been aware of him for some time, older spirits have warned me of him and I know the true extent of his power. But what I offer him, I'm sure he will take."

"And what if he's more powerful than you? What if he won't listen to you or anybody, after all he's been unstoppable for many years," I interrupted our angry silence, but Gabrielle stayed woefully calm. I knew her decision had been made.

I looked at her incredulously, her beautiful pale face staring down towards the courtyard, her lips painted so delicately red. The black lace of dress shifted in the wind, and then came the gunshot.

Amon had shot the young dealer in cold blood as he'd turned his back and prepared to leave the scene. Amon quickly ran over and searched the body, looking increasingly angry when he realised that something was missing. Snatching the dealer's wallet, the killer fled over the wall and off into the night.

I watched him escape with fury in my eyes, the dealer lying in a pool of blood, the same way I had been left struggling for life what seemed like a decade ago. Instead of waiting for his eventual death, Gabrielle turned her back and disappeared from my side, without uttering another word.

I stayed there for a few minutes longer, upset that Alex would risk his life just for me – what had I done to deserve his love? I felt lost, unable to process the information that had been so eloquently put forward by Gabrielle.

She was cold, unfeeling and selfish; what she wanted was dangerous and her confidence didn't deter from that fact. Once his soul was let loose, how could she know that she could control it, harness it for herself?

I hated him with every part of my soul, I'd never felt such strong emotions of disgust before. But I realised I was also still scared of him, the power he possessed.

And of course there was the question of how this monster could ever be stopped. Her words were sharp like a knife and she had predicated Alex's death. As questions spiralled through my mind I felt I had no choice but to co-operate.

I stayed with Alex until early morning, thankful that he was safe and deep in sleep. I watched his motionless slumber, perpetually undisturbed by ghouls or nightmares. I had always envied the predictability his sleeping patterns.

He looked like an angel, sleeping soundly with one arm over his pillow, the other by his side. His hair was long and scruffy; he still hadn't bothered to cut it. I sat on the bed next to him, holding my legs close to my chest in an almost childlike way. He slept in his boxers, and I admired his perfect skin as I thought about Gabrielle's offer.

"You need to get on with your own life," I whispered as he lay still, his breathing light and even. Sometimes it was hard to remember there was a thin wall separating me from him, that he couldn't hear a word I said.

I smiled, feeling his warmth in the only way I could anymore, unable to move away from my old flame. Still, Gabrielle's words echoed in my mind and I knew that soon I would have to make a decision.

With a sadness I realised I would do anything in my power to protect Alex, but my power was limited.

Night dissolved into morning and the light started to trickle into the room as sadness trickled into my heart. I started to fade into the background, forcibly separated from an oblivious photojournalist.

Chapter Nineteen

That's when things started to go wrong. I woke not to find myself in the darkness of Magnus's old room, but instead in a small office almost void of detail. The walls were dark green and in the corner there stood a small table and pot plant. I was sitting in front of an oak wood desk.

On the ground lay the body of a man I did not recognise; he wore a black suit and blue patterned tie. He was mid-thirties, had blonde hair and his eyes were lifeless, staring up at the cream-coloured ceiling.

But it wasn't me; it was as if I was seeing the world through someone else's eyes – a man's eyes – and straight away I realised that it was in fact Amon.

It was like a dream; I had no control over the situation as he rolled up his sleeve and retrieved a needle from the same briefcase that he'd been carrying the night before.

It seemed Gabrielle had been right about his drug addiction. His arm was covered in small bruises and marks as he got to work with the tourniquet and needle. I wanted to turn away as I saw him inject into his damaged veins, and growing even more alarmed I realised it was day. His watch read 11:34am.

I could feel his body start to shake, the feeling was surreal and my confusion deepened. It felt I had become his eyes, if only temporarily and I was completely powerless to stop him or interfere with his motions.

The papers on the nearby desk had been disturbed, but there was nothing unusual about their contents – accounts mostly. Our exact location was bothering me – I had no idea where we were or even if we were still in London. I grew impatient with him, my disgust growing at having to witness these crimes.

The rush of the heroin was taken hold of him and I felt it too, unable to intervene or move in any way. Part of me hoped he would die right there and then, but gradually the shaking slowed and he seemed to gain control of his body once more.

I realised I could feel a deep, powerful rage deep down inside and I knew it was his rage; probably built up over many years it was impossible for me to comprehend the extent of the damage he had already done to the world.

Perhaps Gabrielle was right; he was better off dead, but the thought scared me. As a spirit, what was he capable of? He looked pathetic to me as I watched from his point of view, struggling to his feet.

Eventually he put away his tools, rolled down his sleeve and put on a pair of black leather gloves, hands still shaky, checking to make sure the door was still locked before taking the wallet he'd stolen from the dealer. Looking inside it held cash and a driver's licence for Lorne De'Vanquer – probably fake.

He took the cash and placed the wallet underneath the pot plant, quickly scanning the room for anything he'd left behind before unlocking the door and making his way down a long red corridor. I could hear loud music playing in another room, and I realised we were in a bar.

Stopping at a mirror, I saw the stolen face that had once been Petri's in full light of day – it was now scarred and worn looking, the eyes dull yet cold and staring. He looked uglier, skinnier, as if he had neglected to eat properly in weeks. His hair was slightly longer, and today he wore a grey suit which he straightened up wearing the gloves.

There was no blood on the suit, nothing to make him conspicuous to others yet I wished someone would stop him before it was too late to notice the guns hidden in his suit.

Amon turned towards the nearest door and entered the bar, which held only three single people standing in the shadows. It was unusually quiet which made me consider that it was not open to usual customers. Amon's mobile phone started to ring.

I watched as he fished it out of his pocket and snapped it open, his voice creepily deep he spoke, "Yes, you have the information?"

I heard a man's voice reply, "I might have something of use, meet me tonight at 11:30pm at the location we agreed upon."

"Are you sure this is right? I need the item urgently, do you understand me?" Amon snapped, sounding impatient and frustrated.

"I'm positive," was the reply, to which Amon hung up the phone and placed it back in his jacket pocket.

I had a feeling that whatever was going to take place that night would be exactly what Gabrielle had warned me of. It was the reason I was there, watching through Amon's eyes.

Now I had a time, all I had to do was follow Alex to the meeting point and protect him the best way I could – and watch the scene play out. The thought terrified me, having so little control over Alex's life and exposing him to danger.

As Amon shifted in his chair, I had a feeling that my new bond with the killer was not over yet. I was right when I caught a flash of his intentions. Panicking, I already knew there was nothing I could do to stop him. I had to watch until the horrible scene played out like it was supposed to.

Amon stood up and with an overall feeling of invincibility, took out twin pistols and fired shots across the room in quick succession. The guns were loud and vibrated through the room, making me feel almost physically sick.

I briefly saw the first two victims fall to the ground, one clasping his lower torso while the other had a shot to the head. I saw the first had been gut-shot, and was screaming in agony before Amon stepped forward and also shot him in the head with a cruel ruthlessness that he had no doubt developed during his reign of immortality.

Blood splattered across the carpet, making me want to recoil in shock but thankfully I was spared the sight soon enough. He wasn't finished yet.

Amon then turned to face the man behind the bar, who was shouting not to shoot with his hands out in front of him.

"Get out, run you have five seconds before I shoot you," Amon instructed calmly but firmly in the same accent I had heard on the phone just moments before. It had a strange quality, he spoke with a deep finality that I could not place.

"No, wait!" The barman shouted, his arms waving around in panicky motions.

"Too late," Amon replied.

The barman was Asian, balding with dark hair, and I saw the fear in his brown eyes before the shots seemed to blow out in slow motion. Soon he was also on the ground.

Then we were running towards the exit, guns holstered and zero alarms. Just before he stepped out the door he removed the phone from his pocket and dialled number 2 on speed dial.

"Hello Fay?" He asked, his accent thick and deadly serious.

"Yes, you require assistance?" A female voice asked.

"Send a taxi to Klein Street, have it pick me up in exactly fifteen minutes."

The street outside was bright and full of people, with no knowledge of what had just happened in the bar. As he uttered those last words, the scene around me started to fade in the same way as usual and I realised my time with Amon had come to an end. Before I was pulled out I sensed the great power he'd possessed in the many years of life on this world. He was a very dangerous individual.

All of a sudden I was surrounded by coldness as if I was being pulled back sharply, sucked into darkness. It wasn't quite pain, but the coldness was so sharp I was unable to think as a sensation of pins and needles took over me.

All I wanted was for the feeling to disappear, and then it did. With a sensation of vertigo I realised I was back in the darkness of Magnus's room, the darkness almost pitch black like an unrecognisable void. Then I realised I was not alone.

At first the darkness was indistinguishable from the cold sharp surroundings that pulled me in like a suction wave, but then slowly objects became clear and my thoughts soon began to make sense again.

I looked searchingly into the darkness, the feeling of being watched failing to disappear like everything else. I tried to move, but almost fell over in a dazed blur that only confused me more.

"What is this?" I called out to anybody who was listening, still unable to fathom how I could be affected in this way. There came no reply

Just as I looked towards the mirror I saw a black shape dart across the outskirts of my vision. Turning sharply towards what I thought I saw, I felt cold.

"Gabrielle, what have you done to me?!" I cried, sure now of the cold awareness that had been in my presence. Yet still there was no reply.

I waiting in the dark, still and silent. I soon realised I sensed no being, no disturbance to the room; I was alone.

And then I crouched down on the floor, my hands over my head and I screamed loudly - with no expectation of salvation; no rescue, no reply. None came.

In that small time, I tried to feel myself again - it was as if I had to reach down inside myself and just pull out what I knew. Time was now absolutely precious; I couldn't afford to think about what I'd been just through and the consequences of my actions.

I had to tell myself repeatedly that it wasn't me - wasn't my actions. I was muttering to myself, trying to make the memories fade yet I felt stuck in a loop, seeing the barman's face repeatedly as it exploded in a flood of blood and skull.

I pulled myself out of it, had no choice as time slipped me by.

Chapter Twenty

When I finally pulled myself together I went to visit Alex, already knowing that it might be too late and hoping beyond hope that he hadn't left his apartment.

It was still early but I knew that if he'd already left it was unlikely I'd be able to track him down in all of London, and when I finally did it would be too late.

When I got to his apartment I felt enormous relief when I saw his familiar figure in the window. He was silent, his mood at first difficult to pick up on. My relief was soon quelled when I realised he was packing his camera equipment.

Alex had never possessed a weapon - it wasn't in his nature. I had resigned myself to the truth: that Amon was dangerous and well-prepared and whatever was going to happen would mostly likely finish tonight.

I knew from Gabrielle that once the events had started, they would play out whatever I did to try and stop them; it was nature. I wished she was wrong, and summoning all of my strength I prepared to do my best to prove it.

Her words came back to me as I followed Alex around the apartment, the charm still tied around his neck like a sacrifice for the monster. I wanted to make him remove it; if only he knew what it meant and the true extent of this creature's crimes.

My heart filled with sorrow and I whispered as I watched him there, "It doesn't make you closer to me, only closer to him."

He had stopped at his desk, and for just a moment he seemed to look as if he was listening for something. I never entertained for one second that he could ever have heard me, but then I got a shock.

"Night?" he called, sounding confused he turned around to look at the empty room. There was a slight look of worry on his face. I stood there, too shocked to even move as the moment seemed to last a lifetime.

Slowly he walked towards the sofa and sat down with his head in his hands. Shaken but curious, I slowly moved closer to him, assuring myself that he could not have heard me.

As if in response to my silence, he said, "If that's you, I bet you don't want me to go. Do you?"

He looked up to the ceiling, as if thinking about the madness of the situation; probably laughing at himself for talking to the dead.

I took a deep breath, and deciding to test him I used all my emotion built up inside, "No, Alex don't go, please! It's too dangerous, stay away from him!"

Even though I stood facing him, shouting loudly and my hurt cutting me like a fresh wound, his face didn't even flicker. I was exposed, but it was as I thought; he was unable to hear me and this had never changed.

With sadness it dawned on me that it gave him comfort to think I might still be there, and it unsettled him that his actions might also make me unhappy.

He was still unmoving in the chair, so I knelt down in front of him and put my hand over his - again he did not flinch but instead moved his hand away to wipe tears from his face before standing up and walking straight through me.

I watched as he tried to pull himself together before throwing on his jacket and I accepted that he really was going to go through with it.

I had to keep my fear in check as we walked into the cold night air. It was surreal; walking with Alex through London like so many times in the past. I could have entertained the idea that we were still together, yet there was a large invisible force-field between us that kept us apart and me forever lost from him.

I felt like his protector, his guardian and it struck me that maybe that's why I was still there with him. It occurred to me that maybe after this night I would have no reason to stay in this world, the same way Magnus had lost his wife.

We passed many spirits, the streets seemed to be unusually crowded with the dead; many of them staring straight at us - at me. Others were lost in their own dazed and confused state, as many a lost soul I'd witnessed on the streets of London.

But it seemed like every strong spirit we passed had their eyes on me, making me want to shiver right down my spine.

A soldier in uniform, scars down his face and rips down his torso approached from the middle of the road. His eyes followed us as we passed, increasing my paranoia.

A middle-aged woman, dressed in 80's style clothing walked towards us on the pavement, in-between two teenage girls who had no idea of her presence. Her eyes seemed fixed on me, almost bore into me until we had passed. When I looked back, she was walking backwards still facing me.

I tried to ignore them the best I could, as we walked on through streets I didn't recognise. Alex was cold but walked strong and fast through increasingly deserted areas of town and I began to grow fearful for him.

He reached into his pocket as his phone started to vibrate, and picking it up he answered with, "Tell me where I'm going."

He nodded as a voice spoke into the receiver and I realised it must be Alex's source. It was something I hadn't thought of, how he'd managed to track Amon down so easily.

"What about you? Will you be safe?" Alex asked the caller.

"Alright, I'll follow." I heard him say before he hung up and placed the mobile back in his pocket.

We walked on quickly, taking many twists and turns as Alex continually looked over his shoulder; I could tell we weren't being followed, that he was paranoid.

Eventually I realised a figure stood at the far end of the street we were in front of - he seemed to be looking out for Alex and when we got halfway the figure started walking away from us. He was about medium height and wore a dark beanie hat, black jacket and jeans. He could have been anybody, probably the reason Amon had picked him.

Alex moved quicker, following the figure up ahead still checking behind him to make sure it was clear. My concern grew when I sensed Amon was near, and soon enough Alex's source had stopped close-by. The meeting point was somewhere up ahead.

Alex moved carefully, silently as I viewed them overhead - they had stopped in a small car park at the back of a small private company. Amon stood lighting a cigarette in the corner, as the source nearby waiting for his signal.

The car park opened out onto a small pathway, cluttered with recycling bins. Alex had stopped, listening carefully but unable to get a good view of the area. I watched as he moved as close as he dared to where my killer stood.

How convenient for him; the item he'd been searching for had been brought to him like food on a plate. If only he knew the one thing he cared about was waiting in the pathway...but then I saw the nod the source gave to the killer towards the passageway and it dawned on me that he did know; it was a trap that Alex knew nothing about, the perfect lure.

In fear and panic I watched Alex slowly inching closer to the car park entrance, his nervous body shaking. I felt sudden anger at him for risking his life for me when I was already dead, what could he possible expect to achieve? He was going to get himself killed and I couldn't watch, realising that Gabrielle's prediction would come true if I didn't do something - anything - I fled the scene.

Leon was sitting alone in library room. His laptop was turned off and he sat doing nothing when my spirit crashed into the room in a sweeping frenzy.

He turned in shock towards the source of the disturbance, but before he could utter a word I'd said it all.

"Leon, I need your help they have Alex! They're going to kill him if we don't do something, please help, you have to help!"

"Who's they?" He asked, confused but remaining calm as he witnessed my flurry of fear.

"Amon! He is the one the murdered me, the body-snatcher! Leon, you don't understand, Alex has the charm and he's being led straight to Amon!"

Looking incredulous he asked, "And what can I do? Just storm in there and demand they let him go?"

"Do you have a gun?" I asked, desperately hoping for the right answer.

"No," he replied, the agony of my silence in the air bluntly obvious. He sighed, and continued, "Okay, but it doesn't belong to me, it's the library's. It's kept on display but the owner, Mr Green is a very old man who believes in keeping it loaded for emergencies."

"Great! I'll draw you a map, you have to help him or I'll never forgive myself for letting him die," I told him.

He sighed, "Nice enthusiasm for my safety, thanks for that."

"I'll try and protect you the best I can, I'm begging you there's no hope if you don't leave now."

"My life is nothing, let's go," he replied, my mind too occupied to properly process his words.

He watched in shock as I picked up the pen and drew him a quick map, telling him I'd help guide him on the way. I was using up a lot of my energy, but I didn't care for at that moment Alex's life was all that mattered to me.

The library wasn't that far from the meeting point, so I watched as Leon prepared to leave the library, my senses tensed as fear rose up inside of me like flames growing bigger and brighter, an unstoppable fire.

He left the library and with paranoia setting in, looked over his shoulder as he walked briskly on the pavement. For a second I wondered what I would have done without him, but the danger was still very real, for both of them now.

Back at the car park, the source was talking to Amon, "I'm pretty sure about this guy, but you'll know for yourself if you decide to meet him."

"What can you tell me about him?" Amon replied, deadly serious.

The source shrugged, before replying, "It's her ex. Likes to take photos. He has an...interesting necklace."

"I see," Amon replied, "And he doesn't know a thing?"

"No sir, he's completely clueless," the source replied. Amon laughed quietly, a cold and evil laugh that made me very angry.

Alex looked confused at their discussion, probably unaware of the true meaning of their words. They kept it just cryptic enough.

"And you're absolutely sure? You know, I'll pay you life money if you get this right," Amon told the source, his accent almost terrible to listen to - he disgusted me.

"Just, give me what I'm owed for now," the source replied, looking uneasy as Amon moved towards him with the same briefcase as earlier, "I don't want to get involved in any of this weird shit."

Amon opened the briefcase, exposing wads of cash in notes, bundled up crudely with elastic bands. The source did not stir, but instead waiting on Amon selecting the right amount and handing it over discreetly.

Alex had moved even closer, taking a very real risk he's taken out his camera and had captured images of the money being exchanged.

At that moment I wished I knew what kind of deal Alex had made with this guy, but he didn't seem bewildered at all by the conversation Amon and the source had just had before his eyes. My heart was filled with fear as I watched these events unfold, knowing that at any moment Alex could be exposed to serious danger.

I grew more confused as I thought about what Alex was doing; why was he there when he knew that Amon was interested in him? Did he know why? It occurred to me that Alex knew that my killer had been searching for something, possibly for him although I reasoned that he couldn't know why or else he wouldn't be putting himself in so much danger.

Growing desperate, in my mind I damned him for being so reckless of his own life. It hurt me that all this was my fault for doing things I shouldn't, taking risks. Still, it was a cruel pay back to watch the situation unfold like this.

The beanie guy had now taken the cash and pocketed it, and now I watched as he said, "Look, give me some distance first."

Amon didn't respond and beanie guy first walked swiftly and then ran towards the company entrance and out of the car park.

The next part happened fast; as he ran, Amon took his hand out of his pocket and I saw one of the guns from earlier that day. The gun had been silenced, but shots went off fast and beanie guy fell to the ground.

Alex recoiled quickly, started to move back towards the path before Amon called out, "I know you're there! If you run now, you're dead!"

Alex froze, his face a deathly pale as I watched Amon move towards the back entrance to the park. He put the gun away and smiling, he held up his hands.

"Look, no gun. Now come out, come out, wherever you are," Amon crudely sang, loudly and impatiently.

Alex seemed to hesitate and then with horror I watched as he stepped forward, out of his cover and straight in front of Amon. He stayed silent, watching as the killer's smile widened.

"Come closer, let me look at you," Amon said, his voice mellow and carefully hiding his rising stress levels. As a spirit, I could tell he was growing increasingly desperate for the charm that I'd taken from the beach; his immortality. Poor Alex.

"W-what do you want from me?" Alex stammered, as he took a step closer. I felt helpless as Amon walked right up to Alex and reached out at his neck.

Alex, surprised jumped back before stumbling and falling down to the ground. Amon laughed, his eyes looked wild and almost incoherent as he approached the terrified Alex. I couldn't stop it anymore, before I knew it I was on ground level but with little energy there wasn't much I could do.

Alex tried to get up but Amon was getting closer. I saw him stick his hand in his jacket pocket as if to retrieve the gun and growing infuriated I pushed him back like a strong gust of wind while Alex stood up in panic.

Amon stumbled but didn't fall, disconcerted for just a second before shouting, "You can't escape here alive!"

Alex looked scared, but he stood his ground and surprised me with his outburst.

"You killed her, you fucking killed her you bastard! Why, what the fuck did she do to you?! Why did you do it!"

His voice was full of anger, his face stricken with grief but his words fell on death ears. Amon laughed, before replying, "You are nothing to me! She was nothing! You are a fool to think you can avenge her death, but I'm glad that you tried. Very convenient for me."

Alex, out of breath and weak looked scared as Amon approached him and, unable to run he stood his ground bravely. I looked on in terror as Amon released some sort of primal cry and brought out a knife that shined darkly for just a second, before it entered Alex's chest with brute force.

"Nooooo!" I screamed, but my voice stayed unheard.

Alex's eyes grew wide as Amon reached for his neck and snatched the charm, breaking the leather band that held it in place. He was almost grunting in excitement as he held the charm, reunited the way he'd dreamed of.

All of a sudden Amon paused as a gunshot ricocheted through the car park and almost in slow motion I watched as the charm fell out of his hand and landed on the ground. Then Amon joined it, staring into space as part of his head lay in small pieces on the wet ground.

Looking towards the source of the shot, I was glad to see Leon standing there in his dark jacket. He looked pale and smaller than I remembered.

"Leon, quick, call an ambulance!" I cried as I ran towards Alex. He was still breathing although lightly.

Leon nodded and soon he was gone, leaving Alex and I alone in the cold darkness. I used all my energy to try and keep him warm; he was drifting in and out of consciousness and all I could think of was the last time we spent together, all warm in bed with his body against mine. It hurt to think of that time.

I wished to God that Amon's eyes hadn't been spared from the gunshot; they stared out blankly but still they looked full of haunting evil.

I tried to rock Alex awake in my arms, but it was draining my energy badly; I was weak. I knew it was only a matter of time but then the nightmare came true.

Amon started to get up from his body. At first I didn't move; I stayed with Alex as I watched the dead man stand. Only it wasn't the same dead man at all; he was larger with long, thick hair and dark skin. What shocked me most was his face; twisted, almost deformed it seemed to change significantly with each look; one minute evil, the next looked more like the true man he'd once been. His eyes stared out darker than anything I'd ever seen and I realised that this was the real Amon.

His soul looked ageless; it was difficult to tell how old he really was, impossible to distinguish. His muscles shone darkly, his powerful mass of spirit body looked almost giddy as he got his balance.

Almost immediately he looked down at the charm on the ground, and then to his murdered corpse with zero expression on his otherworldly face; he looked sub-human.

Slowly, he bent down to pick up the charm but when he realised he couldn't, he let out a loud scream that sounded guttural, terrifying in strength. I didn't move, but he must have seen me from the corner of his eye because he turned around sharply to face me.

Cautiously, I left Alex's side and stood up to face him. Shaking, I looked him in the eye with pure hatred and he in turn with rage; his eyes seemed to bulge out of their sockets.

I could tell he was much stronger than me, and with little energy I turned and fled with Amon strongly on my tail. Panic filled me as I realised he was following me, although what he intended to do I had no idea; assured, it wouldn't be nice.

His eyes looked almost insane, burning with anger for everything in the world and his spirit felt hot behind me - actually burning like fire. But I couldn't think about that, my mind was a blur as I tried to get away from his terrible presence.

I sped through the streets in terrified panic, unable to think or process which way I could turn to escape his claws. I could hear him, deep breaths directly in my ear he sounded like some sort of immortal devil - only now he could never be immortal again.

His strength and speed were overpowering to me, my abilities were void to his huge mass of evil.

Suddenly I felt pulled back like a strong wind had grasped me and thrown me for what seemed like miles and then he was on top of me as we fell through the air, what could pass for eyes bearing down into my soul.

His face was twisted into pure evil but each feature blurred into one, each expression more horrifying than the next. His mouth opened to look like a large gap in the shape of his head and I saw large teeth that were menacing and terrible.

It was then I knew what he wanted to do and I started to feel his strength suck me up inside him. Pain pulsed through my body as I tried to resist him with all my force but I knew then that it was too late.

Suddenly I felt a cooling at my side and I realised it was Gabrielle; her blurred spirit almost took on the properties of water beside me and I felt safe under her powerful wing.

I looked at her, confused and for a second, she glanced back and I saw the calmness in her eyes. In that second, I knew what to do and I broke away from him.

Then she turned her power to Amon and the two spirits clashed brightly, almost like an explosion of personalities.

Then I felt like I was drowning. A large crowd of spirits surrounded me completely, filling up every space until all I could see was clouded. She'd called in her army, every single one of them and they were headed for Amon.

I heard him scream but he was too powerful and pushed them back one at a time. I was thrown from side to side in the mass of souls around me. He was causing disruption in their ranks, as I saw individual souls fly through the mass crowd like small explosions in the greyness.

Then I saw through the large cloud; it was the bright light of Gabrielle - it was magnificent, almost blinding. But Amon was controlling her power with equal strength and I saw that she was in trouble.

Around me, some of the spirits seemed to be sucked away violently and I heard their cries when it dawned on me what was happening. I saw its mass in the distance, separating the many spirits from each other with dark force. Some of them were sucked into its power as it moved ruthlessly towards the fighting pair.

"Gabrielle, let him go! It's coming for him!"

The dark void was unstoppable, sucking up spirits in its path as it moved towards the battling spirits. Amon was unpredictable, not wanting to listen to reason as Gabrielle fought him off. The sounds coming from his spirit sounded darker and more powerful as he sucked energy in bursts from Gabrielle.

Just in time she broke free, the darkness sucking in Amon and for a second, I thought he would get away as his power seemed to build with his fury. Then he was swallowed up into the almost conscious large black mass that moved with electric motion.

Gabrielle looked on, her expression unreadable as at first, it seemed to move towards her. Her eyes stared deep inside the silent void and for a moment I thought it would take her and every spirit around me.

Its violence was terrifying and once I saw it, I knew that I never wanted to experience what I had felt before - my energy was low and I wasn't sure I'd be able to fight it.

A sense of relief filled me as it started to move away and then down into the depths of the underground, the deafening electricity in the air slowly becoming bearable.

But as the noise faded, something caught me off guard. It was the cries of a baby – just for a moment I could control and fell to the ground - and then the noise was gone.

The spirits split apart and almost exploded into the sky, directed into every corner until I was alone with Gabrielle. At first, she looked calm as she stood still, elegant as always. Then her eyes met mine and she stumbled, her weakness finally showing through her strong exterior. The surprise in her eyes told it all and despite being weak I put my arms around her and held her still.

She moaned, unable to speak at my gesture but holding to me fast like a powerless child. I felt stripped of the guard I'd set up against her, my sadness raw seeing her so vulnerable and exposed. I closed my eyes and felt the movement around us; when I opened them again, we were back in the car park.

I let go of Gabrielle and cradled Alex, his breathing shallow and his body cold. I held him as warmly as I could until eventually the sirens grew louder and we were joined by a team of paramedics.

I watched numbly as they took over his care and gradually I realised that he would be all right. I felt a hand on my shoulder and turned to see Gabrielle, her face stricken with grief.

"What..." I started, unable to understand what I was seeing. Her eyes were dark with smudged eyeliner, she looked surprisingly like a teenage goth.

"Your love for him is...remarkable," she said with a shaky voice, and I realised that she was crying only the way spirits can. I didn't think it was possible for her to cry, or to show emotion and that's what shocked me so much; it really brought home the extremity of what had just happened.

"Why couldn't I have felt like that? My life was such a fucking waste..." She started to fade into the background, slowly leaving me and I wanted to shout at her to stay. Something kept me from speaking and I couldn't find the words to reply to her. Finally I thought of something to say.

"I'm sure that's not true," I told her, "you're not a monster - you're not like him. Your life must have been filled with colour and beauty."

My admiration for her shined through in my words, and she smiled the faintest of smiles before whispering, "I killed any feelings that I once had, ignored them and left them to starve without nourishment until I felt like an empty shell inside; something I could never admit to anyone, the same wicked smile always there, hiding my real face."

Her bright red lips suddenly did smile, wide and almost carnivorous in the darkness. She reminded me of the Cheshire cat as she faded into blackness, the smile staying all the time.

With that, she left the car park and I stood watching the darkness where her wild beauty had slowly disappeared into nothingness.

Chapter Twenty-One

I remember his smile as I sat in the passenger seat of our old Suzuki that day long ago. We had almost finished decorating the new apartment; our very first place together, it was humble but to us it was perfection.

The last of the furniture had arrived earlier that morning, and in our car we had the last of the boxes to be moved. Then finally, the moment we had been waiting for when we could close the door and for the first time, be home.

It was easy to see the excitement in each others eyes as we drove towards our new street, still several minutes away in South London.

"So, what shall we do first?" Alex asked, his eyes glimpsing me as I faced him the way I so often did when we were driving together. He told me that he didn't like it, that it unsettled him for me to stare that way but it was something I couldn't help but do. He was so perfect, it was incredible to believe that he was mine and we would be living in our first flat together. To be honest I thought it would never happen.

"Well..." I replied, a hint of naughtiness in my voice, "I think we should christen the place."

"How do you mean, like open a bottle of champagne by smashing it against the foyer wall?"

"Hmmm...not quite, darling."

My smile told him everything, and at once I knew that he'd got it; couldn't possibly have missed it, really.

I still remember him clearly that day, the almost boyish glee in his voice, the way his fingers tapped in excitement on the steering wheel from time to time.

His hair was going through a longer period, and he wore a light blue sweater that made me think he looked cuter than he really was. Some light stubble scattered his chin and I traced out every detail and contour of his face, the way I had often done in the past. It helped me to remember him when he was not there. Maybe it was girlish of me to hate every second we were apart, but it felt like sometimes our relationship was on a knife edge; like any point could be our last.

Maybe it wasn't healthy, but it didn't taint our love in the slightest and every emotion for him felt like it could never be heightened by anyone else. He was the one, I was sure of it.

My hand reached out to grasp his as he held the gear stick and he shot me another look which was filled with pure love. I remember thinking that this was it; we'd made it, we were grown-ups and no-one could stop us now.

To everyone around us - on the outside - we seemed like the perfect couple. Yet that had not always been the case.

It was hard to imagine that we were actually doing the one thing that everyone around us had fought against, back when we were clueless teenagers. They didn't believe us, that we'd found love at such a young age and now we were proving everybody wrong. It felt so good.

When we arrived at our destination, we went to grab the boxes in the back like schoolchildren on an excursion to a chocolate factory. Each box contained the smallest of memories; all the big stuff had already been taken care of by my parents, who had seen to it that we would be comfortable on our first night...as I planned it, we would be more than comfortable.

We grabbed everything in one go, just desperate for the few seconds where we would finally lock up and find ourselves in our own little world away from the rest of the busy city.

The boxes were left in the hall as we fell all over each other, then him lifting me through first to the bedroom, before seeming to change his mind and turn me in circles.

"Where to first? Bed? The couch? How about the kitchen?? Tell me, quick! Make a decision or I'll drop you right here and ravish you on the floor!"

I laughed, hysterical as he eventually laid me down on the bed and kissed me with so much passion it made me flush with lust almost straight away.

That night we fed our hunger until we could move no more, completely spent we lay facing each other on the king size bed.

"Could this be any more like heaven?" I asked him, and as he stroked my hair I realised I actually meant it.

Over the years our love had deepened into the most beautiful of understandings and I imagined that we could feel the other's thoughts like a kind of magnetism that existed simply in our bond together.

Being a writer I suppose I did romanticise a little bit, but I saved those thoughts up like precious memories that later comforted me in times of struggle.

That's why I found myself once again thinking of that day, and wondering what the hell happened to us after that.

That first night in our apartment, I woke up thinking that Alex was in bed with me and reached out to him, still content in the warmth of our new bed. I almost revelled in the luxurious fabrics, the little nest we had created for ourselves.

When I reached out to find nothing, I realised something was wrong. I squinted in the darkness and then I saw the masculine figure, standing in the corner of the room like almost a statue.

"Alex?" I called softly, wondering if he was awake. Nothing, silence came the reply.

"Alex...come back to bed, yeah?" I spoke, louder this time so that it was impossible for him not to hear.

Still he stood, facing the blank wall.

Then slowly, he began to turn towards the bed, almost unnaturally at first. It was almost like he was caught on a hanger, strange as that may sound.

"Were you sleepwalking?" I asked him, a note of anxiety creeping into my voice as he had so far failed to answer me.

And then his body seemed to change, to relax as if the hanger had been taken away from him. He stood in his boxers, and slowly he moved his hand up as if to shield his face from sunlight that didn't exist.

"Night? Where are you, God don't leave me," He spoke, a deep sorrow in his voice that I couldn't understand. He seemed to be upset at something in his sleep, and realising it was nothing but a dream I found myself pushing out of bed to approach him, my voice reassuring.

"Hey, it's alright, I'm here," I said, hoping for a reaction. By this time I was feeling a little bit creeped out by his behaviour.

"No, it's not really you. It's a ghost, leave me alone! Bring back Night, she's the only one I need."

I stood back, shocked and firstly unable to speak as his words made no sense to me; but then they wouldn't, dreams are like that.

His voice changed and suddenly it sounded deep and unrecognisable; alien to my ears.

"Get away," the voice said, "Get away, fast. You are not supposed to be here, he is not your final destination...Night, where is Night?"

"No, it's me!" I touched his shoulder, fighting with my instincts, arguing that it couldn't possibly be anything other than a dream.

At first he did not respond, but then I touched him harder, trying my best to provoke him to wake up and suddenly he did, jumping back and making a small sound of surprise.

"Honey, relax! It was just a dream, okay? Just a dream," I told him, incredulous that I'd first had to deal with that on this very night. Why couldn't it have been any other night?

"W-what? What happened?" He asked, sleep now in his voice he was looking around the room, confused and disorientated.

"You stood up and were talking in your sleep," I told him, laughter starting to creep into my voice more out of nervousness than humour, "Do you remember what the dream was about?"

"Fuck, no...wait," he said, as if thinking he put his hand up to his hair and brushed it away before continuing, "no, it's gone. Was it bad?"

"Yeah...it kind of scared me," I replied, unsure whether to tell him the extent of words he'd spoken.

"God, I'm sorry babe," he said, sounding guilty but not so scarily disconnected, "let's get back into bed and forget about it."

Shivering I helped him back into bed, and he didn't mention it the next day. In the morning it seemed like a vague dream, although I knew deep down it was real; it lurked in my mind like a monster in the cellar but I keep it locked up, until the feeling faded.

Only later, after the incident with Amon, when I sat thinking of these memories for comfort's sake, did it send a chill straight through me.

Alex never sleepwalked again, as far as I'm aware. At least in my company, he always slept soundly, like a log. Occasionally we'd bring up the situation at parties or houses of friends, but I had not thought about that time for many years.

I argued with myself, that it couldn't possibly mean anything yet something stirred within me all the same. And then, later that night, I lost the baby.

Chapter Twenty-Two

I stayed with Alex in hospital, noticing every slight change as his condition gradually stabilised. All I could think about was my guilt, seeing him lying there on the cold ground, his life draining out as his blood spilled on the concrete.

The first night was the worst, as doctors and nurses rushed to try and save his life. The operating theatre was tense and I stayed with him through it all, watching from the far corner of the room.

The hospital was a place of death: spirits roamed endlessly down the corridors or lay crying hysterically in the white rooms. I wasn't made to feel welcome there, which was spelled out to me when I was approached by an old man with difficulty walking.

At first, he looked normal as he held onto his walking frame, but it was easy to tell that he was in fact dead. His eyes were small and surrounded by large wrinkles; they stared at me coldly. He wore a grey cardigan and pale blue shirt, that had stains down the front.

"What do you think you're doing here?" He asked me, rudely but before I could answer he was closer yet, his lips marked with spots. His voice was rash and angry, and I could tell he had difficulty pronouncing his words - he was missing a set of teeth.

I felt threatened but stood my ground and he - like others - learned to leave me alone. I would not leave Alex for any soul.

At one point I felt his life was fading, I wished with all my heart that he clung on to life. It was too precious to give away. Before he drifted into unconsciousness I'm sure he looked over to the corner where I stood, his eyes seeming to fix on me for mere moments and that was when I knew the frail fabric between life and death was torn.

Later, when he was given his own room I stayed by his bedside every spare moment that I could. On many occasions we were joined by his friends and relatives, cards and flowers almost crowding the small room.

I could hear him murmur, "I want Night...where is she?"

I could tell it almost broke his mum's heart when she had to explain to him again that I was dead. His sleep seemed broken and disturbed at the best of times.

The moments I was alone with him, protecting him were the times when I wanted to cry but fill with happiness at the same time. It hurt me to see him in that situation, but I was overjoyed that he hadn't lost everything; that I hadn't been the cause of his death.

One evening he lay there, his face calm and peaceful as he slept. He looked thin, his hair growing ever longer and his skin beautifully smooth. Like a man, he grew stubble and when he was well enough, he shaved it off again.

I didn't want to see his life cruelly taken away from him the way mine had been from me; never wanted to see that. Even though I would have given anything to have those few last words to him, the last touch...our final kiss, it would have been so selfish of me to do that to him.

It was a love that would never again be brought to life, his days lived out with others and me...well, that was a completely different story now.

I tortured myself in those days, thinking of what might have been and why I'd acted the way I had all those years ago. I now knew that nothing could ever have compared to what I'd had at home, with him.

The last night I sat on his bedside as he slept, the full moon shining brightly from his window when I felt movement around me. I closed my eyes as I felt the sensation of lace and I knew that I'd been joined by Gabrielle.

"Oh Night..." she said, her voice comforting but surprisingly like old times; I hadn't seen her since that fateful night...the battle with Amon where she'd been stripped of everything she held dear. The emotions from that night were still raw in me.

"What are you doing, dear heart?" She asked me, soothingly as I failed to move from Alex, sitting softly on his bed like a guardian angel that had never existed in his life.

"I don't want to leave him," I told her, the guilt in my voice blatantly obvious to anyone caring to listen.

"Shhh," she replied, "You owe him nothing. To be honest, he shouldn't even be here now."

I looked at her then, but words failed me. Her eyes met mine and I saw the same bottomless darkness inexplicably inside her like some living evil that plagued her. A tumour, that's right, I imagined it as an almost conscious tumour growing deep down inside of her spiritual body, inexplicably there.

"We made a deal, remember?" She asked, her words playfully dark as she leaned over me to look at him. It felt almost dirty, and I responded quickly by sitting straighter, pushing her away from him.

"No, you can't take him away from me," I said firmly, my fear showing underneath, "please leave us alone now."

She shook her head, as if humoured by my nightly vigil to my old love.

"But I wouldn't be taking him away," she replied with menace, "I'd be giving him to you."

My face spoke a thousand words and I shrouded round him, protected him the way a frightened animal would do when cornered. She laughed, softly and sadly.

"You cannot stand against me, Night. You do not have the power to do something so courageous."

I stared at her, amazed by her inhuman suggestion.

"Does it mean nothing to you, the way I tried to protect you and the others from that...thing? I put myself on the line, so please do not do this to me - not now. He has a life to live, just like we did...not that you're able to remember such a thing."

She bowed her head solemnly as she took in my words, and so very faintly she whispered, "No, I don't suppose I do. I know what you did for me, Night, but do not give yourself too big an ego; it was not all up to you."

I stayed silent, my guard still up against her impossibly powerful force, my eyes begging her not to take Alex the way she had done to countless others. Eventually she answered me, ending my agony.

"I will leave him alone, but only if you agree to do the same," she replied as she elegantly paced the room. She turned to look at me, her eyes brightly expectant of my answer, "You know, this is not healthy. You need to move on from this."

"That's none of your business, why did you even come here?" I asked, almost angry now at her playful tone.

"Because Night," she told me, "I care about you. You've been too blind to see, but also, I'm not the only one who needs you right now."

I looked at her, confused at her statement but her expression stayed unreadable. Her smile was faint on her smooth pale face, her eyebrows raised.

I didn't want to fight with her, but something told me that however she got her message across, she was there in peace. I sighed, accepting her message and realising that she was right; I couldn't stay with Alex forever.

"You have to say goodbye now," she said, understanding showing on her face as she continued, "Soon you might not be so alone anymore."

With her words only just registering on my face, she walked through the room and was gone, leaving me full of questions and no hope of answers.

Alex stirred under the white sheets and I knew deep in my heart that Gabrielle was right: he no longer needed me, he was now free to go on with the rest of his life. The killer was dead, Alex was all right so perhaps we had all found our happy endings.

I smiled palely in the dark, the moon partially covered by thick clouds. I reached out to hold Alex's hand, and sleepily he seemed to grab hold of me as if I was still alive.

"Alex," I whispered to him, "I have to leave you now darling. I'm going to miss you, I've always missed you..."

He moved his head sharply to the left, as if witnessing a nightmare and I watched his face grow almost tense and then relax again. It seemed like there wasn't much else to say.

I let go of his hand and stood up to leave, part of me unbelieving that I'd be able to go through with it. Where would I go? What would I do next? Questions I was unable to make sense of as I made my way across the room, silently.

Just as I was about to leave, I heard movement behind me, a rustle of sheets. Turning, I saw that Alex had sat up in bed, one arm almost as if he was reaching out for something and it took me a few moments of shock to realise that he was dreaming.

"Night, it's all my fault..." I heard him say, his voice full of sorrow it took be back and I felt unable to leave. Slowly, hesitating I approached the moonlit-bathed Alex one last time and held him in my arms, before whispering the truth.

"No, it's my fault."

In the darkness he seemed to reach for me, his arms around me tightly. My first instinct was to back away, unsure of how it was happening but then I let my shield down, embracing him in his sleep.

"How are you here," he moaned, his breath slightly warm on my body.

"I don't know how," I whispered, and suddenly he looked up into my eyes. It pushed all of my defences out of the window, as I saw the one thing I never expected to see; recognition. The pain in my heart ruptured and there was nothing left to do but just be there for him, and him for me.

I knew that it was nothing more than a goodbye, that we could never carry on in such an impossible, dreamlike state and yet part of me wondered if this had been a gesture from Gabrielle. If it was, I silently thanked her as I held him in my arms and then slowly laid him back on the bed. His eyes looked sleepy and I watched as he gradually drifted back to sleep.

In the morning he'd wake up and remember this dream, probably ponder on it for a few days until it was forgotten, lost in memory and buried forever in the sands of time.

Chapter Twenty-Three

The damage was done. I still can't remember what happened, where I went for the three or four days after the hospital. It went by in a blur, the cities I visited and the places I saw seemed to mix into one big hectic mix of sounds and faces.

I could still feel the nothingness from the black void that tried to suck me in, its mere presence mollifying. I felt like I was still running, from Amon, the void, even from Gabrielle. I wanted to get away from it all, to run away just like I had always done in the past. It was cowardly, but I reasoned it was also me; my way. What else did I have to return to apart from silence and stillness. I was completely out of touch, purposefully separated from everything that I cared about; sectioned off I tried to quarantine myself.

I kept remembering that Amon was gone for good, yet still my fear seeped through me like an echo in my mind. I was confused, scared and still in a deep shock from what had happened to me...to Gabrielle.

I remember that nothing seemed to make sense to me, as I searched frantically trying to find something of meaning, significance or some reason for my existence in the world.

Deep down I also knew that I had left Alex for good, and my soul mourned for all the times we had shared, the love that grew so strong between us for so long and the way it went unnurtured for years after.

I felt myself spiral out of control with no way of stopping it, blitzing through the wind like I was nothing. I had no respect for anything, my thoughts dwindling as I let myself go in frustration, sadness, my own sweet insanity.

The lights blurred around me, the noise of cities fading into the darkness of rural countryside and then through water, burying myself deep in the cool density as a way of escape. The beauty of the sea was invisible to me, and soon I grew tired of effortlessly gliding through everything that was once a mystery.

It bore no relevance to me then, the idleness of my spirit taking to the earth as if frantically searching for something I had lost long ago, and would never find.

Eventually I found myself on the island; the place where my life changed its course forever. Hauntingly, it looked as if I had never left it, the pale sand undisturbed and the moonlight shining down giving it an ethereal quality.

I lay on that beach, staring up at the stars and thankfully alone I waited for no-one. I don't know how long I lay there, it felt like my whole life was carved out in the sand, like I belonged there in some sort of sweet justice.

I stared blankly at the stars in the same way my eyes had stared blankly into nothingness so long ago - the way I'd been after my murder, all life sucked out of me forever I was detached from everything. Underneath it all I suppose it scared me, putting myself into a self-aware coma yet unable to feel a way to slip back into me again.

This time no-one came to my rescue and I didn't expect them to; no scoldings or reality checks from Gabrielle, of course no advice from Magnus and I knew that Leon would never know where to find me.

I imagined he was continuing with his own life, and I wished him good luck with that - the last thing he needed was a spirit of the dead hampering his love life.

As thoughts drifted back to Leon I pictured the last time I saw him, standing at the back of the car park with the gun still held tight in his hand. I remembered he looked different, almost as if he was too weak to stand.

His face had been pale and shiny in the moonlight. I thought I had seen that look before, but was unable to place it when I pressed myself.

I thought of the last time I saw him; running off into the darkness. His expression had been shocked but he remained silent throughout the whole ordeal, the rain slightly obscuring his dark figure. But also there was something else about him that night, something fearless that I found difficult to pinpoint - he was a mystery and would probably remain so.

There was no way Gabrielle would allow such a union between spirit and mortal, the same way I was no longer allowed to protect Alex.

I realised I owed so much to this individual; he saved Alex's life and without him I don't know what I would have done. It occurred to me that perhaps he needed my help now; that was when I managed to pull myself back from the brink of insanity.

As I travelled through the strong winds and cold darkness of this world, I remembered what Gabrielle had said at the hospital. I had been too wrapped up in my wounds to pay attention to her words but for the first time, they worried me.

She said that soon I may not be so alone, but she couldn't possibly be suggesting that I join allegiance with her, so what could she have meant? Again, Leon entered my mind and I raced back towards London, unable to think the terrible truth, even to entertain it for one moment.

The library was dark and silent and almost right away I knew that he was not there - I was alone in the familiar old building that had oddly brought me comfort in my confused times.

A quick check confirmed my suspicions; the small room that I always thought of as Leon's was dark and unoccupied. The laptop space lay empty, dust starting to gather on the desk.

Worry started to set in but then I realised the time; it was 4:09am. Light would soon enter the stained glass windows and I would be forced to retire my search. Calmness settled into my soul as I left the library, sure that Leon would soon return.

After all, a social life was not uncommon for someone living in London and I assumed he had his own flat somewhere trendy and inaccessible to me; in respect for his privacy, I had never asked him much about his time away from the library.

Time passed quickly as I sat on the roof of the building, watching the people traffic beneath me with a newly-acquired patience. My thoughts ran back to my experiences in death, the things that I had learnt and had been taught.

It was then that I decided not to waste these things, as the world would surely keep on turning without me and perhaps this was the one chance I had left. I didn't know why I was still here, but for once I felt hopeful that my soul existed for a reason.

One day that reason would become apparent and all of this would somehow make sense, like a guiding light in the darkness. With pure willpower, I pushed my faded thoughts of horror into the background and instead looked out into the dark night's sky, searching for nothing in particular.

It was mostly quiet, a place to reflect as the sun slowly but surely drew towards the sky and I began to fade into nothing. It was a cruel trick, confined to being a creature of the dark.

Chapter Twenty-Four

The first time something happened between day and night, the point in time of which I shouldn't be aware, I was sure that it was real. I'd seen things through Amon's eyes and it had given me valuable but dangerous information on the future.

However the second time, I'm not exactly sure how to explain what happened. I found myself bathed in sunlight, lying on the hot sand back at the beach I'd just left.

Confused, I stared up at the sun as if to demand an answer but instead I had to shield my eyes from it's brightness. I was wearing the bikini I'd owned back in Thailand, so long ago, before things had started to go wrong for me.

I soon became aware of a far-away figure walking towards me. It was then I knew that this could not be real; that I was in some sort of dream-like state.

Leon was walking towards me and despite the heat, he was dressed in trademark black trousers and a zip-up black ribbed cardigan. His expression was still too far away to tell, but I sensed it was melancholic in nature.

Slowly I tried to stand, finding it difficult to hold my balance on the sand. I felt like I was in my physical body again, as if I'd simply fallen asleep on my travels and dreamt for all this time that I had been dead.

My mind felt warped at that possibility, but all I had to do was look at Leon to realise that it was not true.

"Leon?" I called to him, "What's going on? Where are we?"

No reply, as he continued to walk forward, his face uncovered from the sun. He was walking at a leisurely but sure pace, and that's when I began to feel that something was wrong.

"Leon, what is this? Is that you?" I asked him, unsure of the situation and a feeling of dread only beginning to creep into my mind.

Nervously, I adjusted the strings on my bikini trying to decide if it had really been this skimpy. It was red, with a white patterned flower on the lower half and wooden beads were tied at the ends.

The sea was a beautiful blue colour that seemed all too memorable at the waves slowly crashed onto the sands and when I turned back to Leon I noticed he'd made the halfway point.

I noticed a subtle change around me as it darkened slightly, the waves gradually getting louder and the dark figure continued to walk in my direction. I knew deep down that it was Leon, but something made me think otherwise; made me think of Amon.

Darkness had started to descend on the beach when at first at had been eye-blindingly bright. The waves were crashing violently now and I tried to shout over them with still no response from Leon.

Perhaps he was talking to me, I just couldn't hear him, I reasoned with myself in vain as all of a sudden the coldness sent a shiver up my spine.

The darkness was itself like a wave, sweeping over us so that I could barely see Leon in front of me. I could feel him getting closer and as if in reply to my thoughts a flash of lightning lit up the sky and illuminated his face, making me jump back in surprise.

It was Leon, but his skin was somehow withered and jaundiced, the contours of his nose looked almost hollow and his eyelids drooped down over his eyes, which were no longer a bright blue but more like amber - almost red.

The waves were hitting me now as they crashed over the beach and then suddenly I knew what was coming. It was dark but the waves seemed to die down while the tidal wave made its way towards us.

At the same time, Leon reached out to me and tried to move back when my foot touched something cold and wet. I realised we were surrounded by corpses from the night I'd witnessed the massacre on the island.

I had just enough time to turn back towards Leon, his face now mostly obscured by the dark as I gave him a questioning, confused look, before we were consumed by the sea.

It filled every part of me, overwhelming I felt Leon let go of my shoulder as the powerful tide forcefully separated us.

I could hear nothing, pulled to each side as the water took me in. I couldn't breathe but fortunately I felt no pain, no anguish.

I felt the water fill me up and I realised it was in my lungs, in my throat, in my mouth and then I saw a dark shape floating by me; it was Leon only not Leon. He looked like a corpse, unmoving and dead.

After a while the water seemed to become still and I reached out to him, holding his shrivelled hand like a living person. He did not respond as I pulled him far across the water, until we somehow reached the shore and then I lay down next to him in the darkness, listening to the sounds of small insects and rustling in the undergrowth behind us. It comforted me as I lay there, a corpse with unstaring eyes I was frozen, unable to move my limbs any longer: I was laid to rest.

I was still staring into the darkness when I realised my surroundings were not quite the same; no longer could I hear the water, or the wildlife from the island.

I blinked, and suddenly I could move my limbs; my hands felt the cold wooden floor of Magnus's apartment. My mind seemed to rush with questions, all of which I was unable to answer.

What spirit has dreams? Surely it was impossible, some trick that Gabrielle used to demonstrate her power perhaps? Dreaming was a human trait; I had not felt human for a long time, instead a sub-natural being confined to the outskirts of reality.

The image of Leon's shrivelled body haunted me, the small comforts of 'home' settling me nevertheless. I stared out of the window, afraid of the meaning my dream could have been trying to tell me. I knew something was wrong, and where I had to go.

Chapter Twenty-Five

The wind felt icy and almost violent as it pushed against me. I fought through the weather as the Centaur library beckoned me forward, the hesitation in my mind something I tried my best to ignore.

In the hope that I would find Leon and stop my childish fears I concentrated on him and nothing could stop me, until the old building loomed darkly ahead of me.

Inside it was darker than usual; I sensed very little light as I quickly moved through the upper rooms towards the back. In front of me I could see a candle had been lit, and for a second my hopes rose.

So many confused thoughts entered my mind as I traced through the maze of the library; I felt my nerves heightening almost as if I was afraid of what I would find. The realisation hit me that I was nervous but desperate to see him.

It was then he stepped in front of me, dressed in black I could see his pale face, calm and expressionless in the candlelight. His eyes stared directly into mine and I felt momentary confusion; had he been waiting for me here?

I moved closer towards him but this time I realised it was different; he was looking straight at me, as if he could really see me time, his bright blue eyes registering my movements with something almost like affection.

I smiled from across the room, and a faint smile also appeared on his lips - but it was a sad smile.

"Night," he whispered as he stepped closer to me, his smooth skin almost glowing with something I would have called effervescence. His hands reached out to me, but unlike the dream I felt no fear welling up inside me like a dark panic.

He seemed more real to me than ever before, as if the thin veil of life had somehow shifted and we were closer to each other than ever before. We touched, and I felt what I can only describe as love.

It was like electricity shot through me; his touch. For a second I couldn't think how it could be happening, instead grasping the moment with everything I had, momentarily dropped my anchor of pain and isolation. He was with me.

I stepped back, unable to speak I searched his face for an answer. In shock and sadness I realised what he had done but suddenly it didn't matter, all that mattered was his body close to mine as we held each other for what seemed like an eternity.

When I could finally bring myself to look at his face once more, I still couldn't find the words to say to him.

"No-one told me you would be this beautiful," he whispered, the quiet sadness in his voice detectable only to me.

"H-How?" I asked, and he smiled as I realised I hadn't really made sense. His eyes seemed brighter than ever before, his lips fuller than I'd remembered he took on an ethereal quality that he could never have possessed in life. I wanted to kiss those lips, I imagined doing it slowly at first, and then passionately as my love for him overtook what was left of my spiritual body, all my energy consumed by feelings like fire surging through me.

"The cancer...it had spread. You helped me, Night...I realised that I wasn't scared - to die anymore," his words pierced through me like a knife. Why hadn't I known? Why could he not have told me about his illness? I felt an incredible sadness but also joy that I was no longer alone in this side of the dark.

The reality of the situation slowly sunk in as he stood before me, his spirit almost too perfect that it hurt.

"Where...?" I started to ask, but before I finished I already knew the answer. Slowly I let go of him and stepped forward towards the next room.

The sight I was met with was no less shocking even though it was expected. Leon's body lay slumped over the desk, the laptop shut down for good.

A bottle of medication lay next to the familiar glass that would no longer pass his lips, and to see him there so lifeless made me want to cry and cry and cry. His hand reached out for an invisible object, his eyes unmoving and blank they lay half open.

"Please, let's leave here, okay?" he told me, and I turned to see him standing behind me, a look of worry on his face that soon faded when I took his hand and smiled faintly.

Together we left the library and as we moved through the night air it was the strangest feeling, to share these things with him like I had once shared with Magnus.

His hair blew in the wind and I reached out to touch it, his energy warm and pure to my touch. It was a fragile dream and in my heart I knew it was one I never wanted to wake from.

He was looking at me as if there was nothing that could come between us and I realised it was the happiest I had ever seen Leon Cardew. I was overwhelmed by the one feeling I never thought I could experience again, having been left forever to rot in my own hell. Now it was heaven.

That night we learned so much about each other, ours souls almost entwined with affection and I couldn't bear to think of our separation.

I enjoyed teaching him all the things that I had once learned from Magnus. He was glowing with the possibility of it all, taking to death in a way I could never have imagined. His soul was bright and new; every time I looked at him I found it hard to believe but I knew then that he was in love with me.

We floated through the skies together, never once letting go as we admired the views and spoke of all the things I could never have shared with anyone before now.

"Sometimes I felt like I was going insane with loneliness," I told him, his eyes series as I confessed, "I scare myself sometimes. I wonder why I'm still in this world and for a long time I couldn't find the answer."

"You question things too much," Leon replied, a faint smile appearing on his lips, "you should just accept how beautiful everything is, the world around us - I say we just observe it the way we're doing right now."

"That's so easy to say now that I have you," I replied as he took my hand in his; it felt warm. He was light-hearted, now without the overbearing heaviness of life - the cancer that had somehow come as a surprise to me. Had I really been so obtuse, so blind to the cancer that had spread through his body, affecting him in the most terrible and gradual decay of his body?

"Teach me everything you know, please Night," he said me, interrupting my train of thought. Those words reminded me of so very long ago, when I had first passed over in this world - I had asked Magnus to teach me everything.

"Your first lesson - you can go anywhere in your spiritual body, see anything you like. You can let yourself go wild, places you'd only ever dreamed of seeing in life. You are truly free to feel the winds through your spiritual body and the waters cold waters moving with you, or bury yourself deep within the sand of the deserts."

I led him faster into the air until things became blurred, his trust in me overwhelming as I took him to see my own surprise. Eventually I slowed him down and he looked around in wonder at the deepness and humidity of the rain forest. I don't know why I brought him there, an isolated exotic paradise - a place for us to be alone.

The large, dark rubbery leaves were thick with dew and small insects sounded in the undergrowth as we sheltered under a large tree that looked truly magnificent, with many ancient stories to tell.

Our souls felt wild and primal as we held each other, my eyes fixed on his. There was nowhere else I wanted to be, and eventually when he looked around properly he was in awe of our surroundings.

"This is...amazing," he said, "You are amazing. Why did you take me here?"

"To show you the endless possibilities...you have no constraints now, nothing to hold you back. Not even me."

For a moment he was silent, as if considering the immensity of what I'd just told him, but then he looked back at me with an expression I couldn't place.

"But I want to be with you."

"In that case," I replied, holding back my happiness, "I will teach you everything."

Well, why waste a moment? I was true to my word, teaching him everything I could think of, the power in his body and the danger of other souls.

I started in words as we rested together deep in the dark forest. I told him all that I'd experienced when I first passed over to our side, my teachings with Magnus and the moment where I let my emotions ruin everything.

"Never, ever let that happen to us, you have to promise me we'll be open with each other. In this world, I don't understand why it'd be difficult," I spoke seriously, and he looked back at me with the understanding that made me feel as if we were meant to be together.

"I feel as if all my senses are not just heightened, but changed. It's as if I'm seeing everything properly for the first time. Things look so...alive and vibrant, even though we're in the dark I can feel the life all around me," he told me, his fascination clear in his voice. I remembered when I used to feel that way, and I looked around at the beautiful sight with refreshed love.

"I know, it's utterly magnificent, isn't it? Look at how alive everything is," I replied, and smiling inside we held each other closer.

"Night?" He asked after a while, waking me up from my deep thoughts. I turned to him, waiting for his question.

"I'm curious...will you take me to Thailand, where it all happened? I want to see the island."

I felt dread start to rise inside me, for all I could think of after he spoke those words, was the terrible dream in which I saw his deformed, dead face. The strangeness of even having a dream confused me, but something kept me from telling him why I did not want to go there.

"No...maybe another time, when it's not so raw for me. Right now I want us to have nothing to do with that place."

"Oh...I see. Well in that case, take me somewhere else that is special to you. Teach me there," he said, his eyes glistening earnestly; if he sensed my hesitation, he did not speak of it. I leaned forward and kissed him lightly on the forehead, before he moved his lips close to mine and I leaned back, playfully. He looked at me questioningly, which made me laugh.

First, I brought him back to the place I had learned to love, the room where old possessions had somehow become mine. He followed me with his innocence and when we eventually entered Magnus's room, he marvelled at the things that lay cluttered around.

"My God," he laughed, "What is this place?"

"It is a room left to me by Magnus, my old teacher, before he passed to the light," I told him as he looked around with his new eyes and powerful emotions - the anchor of his body long gone with nothing to hold him back I wondered if he'd have difficulty adjusting.

I could tell he was fascinated by the old books, journals and knick-knacks that had stood the test of time, albeit dusty.

I watched as he first looked at me questioningly, and when I nodded, reached out to one of the books as if to grasp it in his hands. Of course, he missed and his hand moved through it like mist. It had been...unexpected.

"No, do you feel the energy inside your core? You must focus that energy just enough that you can divert it, push it up and then try," I instructed him.

"Oh wow, this is going to be difficult, isn't it?" He laughed, jokingly looking uneasy. As he make further attempts to pick up the book, I found it hard to take my eyes off him - his incredible energy for a soul so new, his determination that almost seemed to shine, even the look on his face. I was transfixed in ways a lot worse than anything I'd experienced at the library for those many times I'd watched him work.

He turned to look at me as with great difficulty, he carved a line in the dust using his index finger. He smiled, a look of great achievement on his face and I smiled back, happy at his new ability. He was like a child, reminding me of my older days of being with a loved one; the time when everything excites you. Discovering someone new in every way until it consumes everything that you do together.

I helped him at first focus on smaller things, like pencils and then a small ornament, slowly building up to bigger objects until eventually, he looked drained.

"I think we should stop for now, let your spirit rest," I told him and he nodded, his back against the wall as he looked at me with affection.

"One thing I don't quite understand yet. You said when your emotions got the better of you, you were able to create fire. That must have been some pretty strong emotions, because I can't imagine ever being so angry. Maybe in death I am still too weak to show that kind of energy," he pondered, as my own thoughts drifted back to the night I had first killed.

"When you are a spirit, all your emotions intensify," I explained, "even the smallest hurt can magnify. Maybe you will never know these feelings, and I certainly hope I will not be the cause of them."

"I should think not, Miss Swallow," he replied. I felt strange at the sound of my old surname; it reminded me of a time when I was once human and...well, normal. Now I cannot remember what normal was like.

All I knew was that I'd never felt so happy as a spirit but underneath, something inside me stirred as I felt the time move on.

"There's something I have to tell you, Leon," I said, catching his attention once more he turned to me with an expression that hid his worry. He took two steps closer towards me, his hands reaching out for mine with a genuine smile.

"Please, tell me," he said, his voice soft and gentle.

"It's approaching day, we have been together almost the whole of the night and soon we must vanish, temporarily."

A small frown appeared on his face, and then it seemed to register, "I think I recall you telling me about this. But why, what will happen to us? I don't want to leave you, Night."

"It will perhaps be frightening at first, but you must remember that I will be there for you on the other side, waiting. It's just like going to sleep, you will wake from it when darkness falls once more," I explained, trying to hide the slightest fears that were beginning to creep into my mind. He didn't seem to notice, instead looking into my eyes with nothing but admiration.

"But I will miss you," he smiled, his comment taking me aback slightly.

"Do not worry, you'll see me again before you know it."

"But darling...I want to look at you forever. Please say something, I want to know what you are feeling," he told me, his words now becoming uncertain at the finality of what I had said.

"Don't think about it like that," I said, soothingly, "You won't know that any time has gone past, although the stronger the spirit, it seems the longer they can stay in the light. No doubt I will be waiting for you in this room when you awake."

With that I was silent, watching, waiting for the sun to slowly arrive and take him away from me, to separate me from Leon. My youngling.

Without understanding, he stood behind me as I stared out of the window, his hands clasping me around my waist he warmed my soul.

I could feel the time slipping away from us but determined to stay strong, I turned to him and kissed him so softly as I felt all of my love build up, wanting to pour out through that kiss as I felt our bodies start to fade in the light.

"You're mine now," I whispered softly, my wicked smile endearing to his loving nature as he held me strongly in his arms, his eyes flashing subtly. He was still unwilling to let go as we caught the last drop of sunlight.

I can still remember the feeling it gave me, of being whole – something I never thought I'd feel again, just like that, spreading all around me.

Chapter Twenty-Six

When I woke it felt like days had passed, instead of mere hours. I found myself once more in the familiar surroundings of the attic room, but suddenly I felt so far away from the place I had been when daylight had come for us. It was silent as I stood in the moonlight and my emotions came to life at the thought of Leon.

I looked around but so far I was alone with the dusty possessions, like old friends. As I waited, I accepted that it was full darkness that surrounded me and thoughts ran through my head like flash photography. Something else began to creep in, like a trickle of darkness I ignored it. I told myself that he would come back, that I would find him in front of me when it was time.

Sure that he would never leave me, I pushed thoughts of Magnus to the back of my mind - the things he had once told me when I was new to the spirit side myself, of spirits that had simply vanished after the first light.

As I looked out of the window, I kept down my rising panic, trying to forget the things that I knew to be true. Still no lights beckoned me as I searched the skies for answers - where was my Leon?

I longed for his touch, his smile, his bright eyes that took on an almost inhuman quality in death. I craved his lips, the lips that I had kissed not long ago as we waited together for the night to end.

As reality started to set in, I felt a deep despair overtake me; somehow I already knew that he was never coming back.

Perhaps it was a false alarm; perhaps his spirit was elsewhere in London - the library, or somewhere in the city, taken in by its charms like a moth to the flame - but deep down

I knew the truth. It was a feeling, something told me that it was so; he was gone.

For two hours I waited in the small room, unable to fathom what had taken him away from me. Who was the judge that chose who to take, why had I been left this way, like a rejected doll? I realised then that I was terrified of the lights although I'd never seen them come for me.

There was an instinct deep down inside me that had at first told me to beware of the lights, but why? I had watched as Magnus had found his time to leave - they had appeared then, to take him away from me forever. I felt no fear as I'd watched him disappear forever from my sight. Had the same lights taken Leon?

Why would they take him, the one chance I had at happiness, and leave me so cruelly alone? Maybe it was some sort of destiny that would leave me here in the same small room to think of my past, but for what?

More time passed and when he failed to turn up I grew angry and finding it unimaginably hard to accept, I left the room in search of my librarian.

I must have taken to the skies like a lightning bolt, desperately searching for him like something I refused to let go of.

I was pulled first to the library like a magnet, but in the place that we had so often met in the past, there was nothing. At first I didn't even recognise it as 'our place'. It was unusually bare, the desk had become just a desk that stood spotless and empty. There was no comforting sight of the laptop, no notebooks or pens and his glass had been left to dry in the kitchen by some invisible character that had stolen it in the day.

My despair gradually increased as there was no sign of Leon in the library that I could find - it was as if he had never existed.

In an immature rage I threw a series of books onto the floor, inexplicably creating a mess for an invisible person, an unknown somebody to clear up in the morning. I took a deep breathe and left the library.

I found myself moments later back at Gabrielle's hotel, in one of the corridors outside her room. The corridor looked deadly silent, empty but I could feel spirits around me; they were cloaked but the atmosphere was thick with feeling. It felt ominous.

The air was cold as I slowly approached her door, ready for a fight. I wanted to demand Leon back, needed to hear it from her, wanted to force it out of her.

I could feel an unwelcoming presence waiting for me inside the room yet something else stopped me from entering. I didn't even know what I was doing there, but then fear and panic flooded over again and I grew desperate to get Leon back. I opened the door and stepped inside.

The room was cold and breezy, the window wide open snow had started to drift into the room. It was a shock, seeing it look so empty and dreary - gone were the luxurious duvets and cushions, the carpet had been stripped and my feet touched the bare wooden floorboards.

"Gabrielle?" I called out, unsure of how to proceed I let my emotions take over once more, "Gabrielle, what have you done with him?!"

I was answered only by the wind; I could feel nothing but isolation and coldness and I hesitated, the urge to leave the hotel became stronger.

As I turned to leave, I felt a disturbance behind me; it was her. Slowly, I turned around to face her and I was reminded of the same Gabrielle that had battled ruthlessly against Amon. Her eyes were soft, her face flawless, filled with purity and sorrow she looked tired. Her dress was still black as night, long and elegant it dragged along the floor almost like liquid lace.

"W-what happened?" I asked her, still waiting for her to speak.

"I want to leave this place, move on," she told me, her eyes meeting mine I felt an intense pain.

"You don't mean...?" I asked, unable to utter the words.

"No, I don't mean. I just don't feel welcome here anymore, I'm going back to Paris, to the theatre."

"Where is Leon? What have you done with him, Gabrielle I need to find him," I told her, my voice intensifying as my words tumbled out. Even as I spoke those words I realised they were final.

The look on her face told me her answer and made me realise the truth that I had been trying to avoid.

"No," I whispered, my pain unthinkable I paced the room, "No, you have him, don't you?! Tell me where he is, I need him!"

Gabrielle looked down to the floor and sadly shook her head, before meeting my eyes with the coldness of hers, her expression hardening.

"You need nobody," she replied, her voice difficult to read, "You know where is he just as much as I do."

I took a step away from her, my eyes searching for her meaning and finding the only answer I wanted to ignore.

"No! I don't know where he is, just like I don't know where Magnus is! Why don't you tell me, Gabrielle, after all you like to play God!" I shouted, forgetting all fear of her I let my emotions go, ripping through the room. She showed no reaction, standing there like a statue.

"You could call it the next stage, you could call it heaven and hell. I've come near it a few times as a spirit, but apart from seeing an overpowering golden light, I can't really say. No-one has ever gone with them and returned," she spoke, calmly as I watched her lips shape every word perfectly.

"But...why don't they take me! I have no desire anymore for...this! And Leon, I want to be with him, that's all I want," I replied, my voice wavering as I soon realised there was nothing she could have done for me.

For a few moments we stood in silence, my head bowed in a deep selfish sorrow, and her cold eyes staying on me every step of the way. Eventually she spoke.

"I'm sorry," she told me. I heard the words, but for a moment I couldn't understand what she was possibly sorry for. And then it clicked.

"You? Is this because of you?" I asked, incredulous at the idea that she could have stopped me leaving this world.

"Me, of course it was," she nodded as I stared at her in silence, her eyes still never leaving mine, "At the start, I kept you here, yes. I was intrigued by Amon, and by your spirit, Night. Take it as a compliment."

"You did what?!" I replied, in shock at what I'd just been told, "How could you do that to me, to anyone?? What right do you have, Gabrielle?!"

And then it seemed to register, and I had to ask the question.

"And Magnus knew?"

"Of course Magnus knew, that's why he took you under his wing darling," said Gabrielle.

It just kept getting worse. Why had I never questioned the way Magnus had been there for me, just waiting from a distance. Had I really thought it was by chance?

"I...I wish he'd told me," I whispered, unable to think clearly as thoughts ran through my mind at lightning speed, my emotions entangled in a complicated web that I couldn't escape.

"He couldn't bring himself to tell you, you were almost like a child to him - he taught you so much before...well, you know what you did. Selfish, ungrateful brat that you were," her words silenced any argument that I could have summoned up halfway through the sentence.

"What...I mean, what do I do now? You said that I wouldn't be so alone but now I feel more alone than ever. If I could somehow get him back..." I stumbled over my words, trying to come to terms with the agony in my heart.

She shook her head once more, and the look that she gave me said it all. I wanted to scream, to collapse in a flood of tears but nothing so extravagant actually happened. I suddenly felt so weak, as if I would fall with the weight of my emotions and then something wonderful happened.

Gabrielle stepped forward and before I knew what was happening I had succumbed to her embrace; warm and strong around me, she held me and I knew instantly that she understood. I felt a jolt almost like lightning and it moved through me like a shock. I realised she was the one constant thing I had at that moment; it was a surprise to think of her like that, the terrifying creature that had held so much power.

She was truly amazing and for seconds I was taken aback by the power of Gabrielle. But deep down I knew that whatever it was that kept me in this world, I had to work through myself. Perhaps one day the lights would return to me, however deluded it may sound to Gabrielle, it was the hope that I needed to cling on to.

I felt a power pulsing through me, over and over again like electricity only it almost seemed sensual, alive and vibrant through my body. My eyes saw things turn darker, and I saw movement in the corners of the room as if things that had before been still, now had life.

At last I stood back, and everything felt somehow different. She stared at me all the same, and eventually I opened my mouth to ask.

"What...was that?"

"My parting gift to you," she answered, "although do not forget, I will always be around to watch over you."

Confused but resilient, I felt sorrow at the thought of her leaving too. At least I could be sure that she would always be bound to this earth.

Seeming to hear my thoughts, she whispered, "I know. You must go now."

With that, I felt her warmth snapped away from me almost violently as she turned and walked away. The last look that she gave me was one of pity, but also love and admiration.

I wished I could be that strong, but my weaknesses shined through as I stood in the empty, bare room with the wind blowing through me. I enjoyed the snow that fell onto the wooden floorboards and shutting my eyes, I remembered what that feeling had been like when I had a physical body of my own.

"I hope you value the freedom that Gabrielle has given to you," a deep voice spoke from behind me, and turned sharply I saw a spirit that I recognised, one of Gabrielle's devotees with shaved hair and pure white skin. I looked at him questioningly, his eyes shone almost amber as he smiled back; he looked almost fearful of coming near me.

Then he was also gone, through the room just like the wind that breezed around us. I stared out of the window after him, wondering if I'd ever see her again in all her glory, if she would be watching me like she said.

Chapter Twenty-Seven

The light started to creep through the windows of the attic room, yet this time I did not fade the way I so expected. My skin stayed solid, almost glowing in the light I looked down at my bare feet that seemed to grow an almost ethereal quality against the dull wooden floorboards.

It dawned on me what Gabrielle had done, and as I fully understood her last gift to me, I wondered what I would find with these new eyes. I had no desire to explore the world in the daylight; perhaps I would simply wait for the mysterious force to come for me the way it had come for so many souls before me...but what if that could never be my destiny?

Now I knew the truth about Gabrielle; she saw the world through both light and dark and now the gift had too fallen upon me. Perhaps now I would find a true balance, something to cling on to in moments of insanity.

I realised that now there was no escape from my thoughts of torment and loneliness and as I looked around the room, I really saw it for the first time.

The old belongings were nothing but junk, the books no longer the bearer of memories; not for me. They meant nothing to me, only Magnus could have treasured such things in death. The old floorboards were covered in dust and I realised that this had been my tomb, was in fact becoming more like one every day.

It had been so long since the room had been blessed with life; the young visitor, the boy with the shock of blonde hair and blue eyes.

I was once that young and curious, what had happened to that? I felt like a fragile bird, trapped in a dark place and panicking to get out. One day I will leave the attic room for good.

And so I wait for answers as spirits come and go. I stay silent now, the workings of my mind forever searching for the one truth in all of this.

Sometimes I look down to the streets below and watch life pass by at a ridiculous speed, praying to the silence for a saviour, one last hope to take me away from this world. But as time goes by it occurs to me just how scared I am of the 'next step', or if my soul will simply just vanish into nothingness. What if there is nothing, just a dull void waiting to suck up lost souls with greed and force.

I've seen friends and foes, met many characters and yes, fallen in love yet I feel like I know nothing more about the workings of this unstable place. I feel like a stranger to myself and I sometimes wish that I could return to the beautiful, dark seas that made me feel like I was one. Yet that would spoil the memories, would it not?

As the days moved on I feel the slow unravelling of the world around me, yet I have no regard for the human things that go on outside the window.

I've learned many a lesson on this side of the dark, but perhaps my deepest lesson is yet to be revealed to me. I know one truth more than any others; that I will stay here on this earth and until it is time for me to leave this terrible, yet beautiful world I will wait.

I wait for that day with quiet contempt, an observer of time as has always been my nature. Perhaps this is my punishment for interfering with life, yet why come up with such a stupid idea as that when I sit here, soaking in the light, my body absorbing power like an invisible, eternal creature.

Before when it was dark, I longed for light, craved to use my new eyes on the world yet I felt locked in night, never to see the bright colours of the sun. Now when it is light, I long for the darkness when I feel truly comfortable.

There is no rest for me, never can I fade into nothingness I must forever face the hurrying world around me. Sometimes spirits approach me with dark eyes, yet I shall sit and stare like stone until they leave me be.

Their brightness stirs around me, as I watch with tainted eyes the movements of young and old souls alike. It's almost like a dance, although an eerie, haunted, translucent structure of light and dark.

But there is no-one to dance with me, for Leon has long left me alone with nothing to cling to for hope. He was my partner, and although our spiritual union lasted only one night, that night meant more to me than anything I could hope to experience in death.

I think of him often.

Of all the things I could have known and seen in this long and lonely death, he was elegant and wild, brilliant and shining like nothing had been before. He had been mine, my true love.

It is the explicit 'humanness' in all of us that strikes me most in this time; the solemn secrecy of Magnus, the way he protected me when I had no-one else. The undending love of Alex, how he mourned until he thought his heart would burst and his suffering would end. Gabrielle; the fragility of a heart so strong, her courage shining through the dark bitterness that she had shrouded herself in for so long. Leon's bravery, he put all others before himself, even when his body was falling to pieces.

Now they are gone, and all that is left is a memory - their distant faces haunting me in the dreams that are almost real. I wonder if Paris has worked for Gabrielle, if the theatre welcomed her back with open arms.

And sometimes, when I sit there alone in my tomb of an attic, I imagine the light is before me. When all is dark, it glows first through the window, a gold shimmering light, and then it moves through the wall, beckoning me.

Slowly I find myself rising up, reaching out to the unknown and then I see him, his face deep gold in the centre of the glow and he smiles at me in a sad way. I get so close that I can feel him, his love for me almost overpowering it makes me want to cry.

Just as I think that I have found my ending, the warmth vanishes and the glow quickly fades to nothing. All I am left with is a vision of his face, turning slowly to horror as he shouts out to me in silence.

Maybe one day the lights will come to me and I will have everything I've ever wished for. Everything I see now will be illuminated and understanding will flush through my heart until every little piece of the puzzle will make sense.

There will be beauty and fusion and my soul will be joined with the one I love. Nothing else will matter and life will continue perfectly in time, like a sort of heaven.

Maybe it will happen.

But still I remain in the attic room, waiting patiently, coldly for warmth to come through and bathe me in its beauty.

I wait with no expectation of a cure for my tired heart, no saviour of light or dark to show me serenity or sense.

Why do I wait? It is a small thing. Something that I lost a long time ago, neither living nor thinking, but mine all the same. But what does that matter now...

My future is uncertain. The only thing that keeps me here, from the earliest dawn to the darkest of nights, is my anchor of hope.

THE END

.

Printed in the United Kingdom by
Lightning Source UK Ltd., Milton Keynes
139822UK00001B/207/P